KISSING
KATE

Genesis –
Happy Reading!
K. Lyn Smith

a sweet Regency romance

K. LYN SMITH

Paperback ISBN: 978-1-7376579-8-9

"I do love nothing in the world
so well as you."

- William Shakespeare,
Much Ado About Nothing

PROLOGUE

BENEDICK KIMBRELL ATTEMPTED to steal his first kiss from Miss Catherine Parker in the perfectly imperfect spring of 1808. But his hopes, then and since, were larger than fact.

At thirteen, he'd been instantly smitten with the demure lass who arrived with her botanist father to pass the spring amongst Cornwall's abundant flora.

She was quite unlike any other female of his acquaintance. Calm and poised. And clean. While many of the young misses of Newford—his own cousins included—sported mud-stained frocks and dew-dampened hems, Kate Parker somehow remained above it all. She, quite simply, defied the dirt.

He'd almost convinced himself she must have been an angel or sea siren, or perhaps, more practically, a princess from some distant kingdom. Indeed, no one in Newford had been surprised to learn she was great-granddaughter to a marquess on her mother's side, though she displayed not a bit of excess pride for it.

All of this was to say Miss Kate Parker settled charmingly atop a creamy marble pedestal in Ben's mind. It had been no small thing when his brother Alfie and cousin Gavin dared him to steal a kiss from the incomer lass during one of their grandfather's Sunday picnics.

While his relations amused themselves with lawn games, Ben walked with Kate on the nearby cliff path that edged the sea. As she admired the wildflowers, Ben collected his courage, rolling his shoulders as he might have done before hefting one of the timbers in his uncle's building firm. But then, as he leaned toward the lass, she knelt to inspect a stem of bluebells, and Ben was left kissing the air. For bluebells!

Kate stood and he quickly straightened, adopting a serious expression as she waxed on about the flowers. Bluebells, it seemed, were her especial favorites. "My father says the bluebells have returned for centuries to the old wood near our home. Did you know their sap was once used to bind books?"

He'd not known such an intriguing fact, and he

contented himself with hearing her tales of the flowers they passed.

That spring, Kate became fast friends with his cousin Bronwyn, one of Newford's dew-dampened lasses, and the pair grew as inseparable as the tide and sea. It followed that Ben spent more time in Kate's company as a result of the acquaintance but, contrary to what one might assume, more *opportunities* for a kiss did not, in fact, assure success.

His second attempt along the stone quay of Newford's small harbor was interrupted when a gull flying overhead dropped a mussel shell between them. Kate jumped back with a soft giggle, and though he counted himself fortunate to hear the sound, his kiss had once again failed the mark.

His third and fourth attempts met with similar success, which was to say none, and by the fifth, he resolved to see the thing done. Spring was yielding to summer, and a noisy crowd—Ben's brothers and cousins included—toted logs and kindling onto Copper Cove for one of Newford's great bonfires. There was a pleasant nip to the evening, and the air round the fire had been filled with mischief and merriment, as it usually was. He'd walked with Kate on the sands, sharing an amusing tale of his younger siblings' latest antics. With a houseful of brothers, he was never without an amusing tale or two.

Kate, who'd never seen the sea before arriving in Newford, loved to watch the waves roll ashore. So, he showed her how, if one's timing were just right, one might walk above the surf by navigating the flat boulders that dotted the beach. The trick was in reading the rhythm of the sea and knowing which boulders would next receive a washing.

"How fortunate you've been," she said as she skipped to the next rock, "to have lived by the sea all these years. Having heard it now, I can't imagine never knowing its sound."

And Ben, who'd never given the matter much thought, decided Miss Catherine Parker must be the most profound young lady of his acquaintance.

As they walked, the noise of the crowd faded behind them. Soon, he imagined they were alone, with naught but the never-ending shush of the waves and the milky light of the moon to guide their path across the stones. Their steps brought them closer and closer still until they stopped to gaze together over the endless black sea. He leaned toward Kate and—

"Benedick Kimbrell!"

Bronwyn's shout caused them both to start. And as he'd been standing on a sea-slicked boulder at the time—one of the very boulders on which he'd just tutored Kate—he slipped to land, soaked and sputtering, amongst the waves.

Kate knelt with gratifying haste to see that he was all right, holding her skirts free of the splashing foam. On seeing he suffered no more than a great thumping to his pride, her smile broke free. There was charm and a soft kindness in her gaze, and his answering grin came easily, despite his dripping hair.

Bronwyn had reached them by then. She stood clear of the lapping waves, hands on her hips and eyeing his soaked attire. "Never say you were trying to steal a kiss," she said.

Her voice carried on the night air, and heat rushed up to warm Ben's neck. He stared at his cousin, willing her to the darkest depths of the sea. Then, to Ben's surprise, Kate came to his defense. "Don't be silly," she said. "My grandmother says only common rogues resort to kiss stealing."

Bronwyn snorted. "Aye, 'tis a sure enough fact. Come, my mother has packed some cakes."

His cousin strode away, arms swinging. Kate hesitated, looking from Ben to Bronwyn and back again, her lower lip tucked behind her teeth. When he thought she would leave him as well, she leaned close. Twin spots of color stained her cheeks as she whispered, "Were you? That is…"

Heat climbed his neck again. He searched his mind for something charming to say. Witty, even, though he would have settled for mildly intelligent.

But he only handed her words back to her. "Don't be silly."

Her lips formed a small O—of relief? Disappointment?—before she hurried to catch Bronwyn.

Despite his mortification, Ben had been an ambitious lad, with hopes that outpaced his reach. He might have recovered. He might have found his courage to attempt a sixth kiss, and a seventh, had fate not stepped in to change his course.

That had been the summer his mother died, and then his uncle. The two of them gone within a fortnight, and a bit of Ben's courage along with them. He didn't see Kate again that year. By the time the funerals were over, she was gone. Returned to her home in Melton Mowbray.

As the months passed, he packed his grief away along with his black armband. In time, he turned his efforts to other young ladies. Kate's family returned the next year, and the year after when her father moved them to Cornwall for good. And though Ben had enjoyed many kisses in the time since, none had ever seemed as sweet as the one he'd never shared with Kate.

CHAPTER ONE

SPRING 1820
NEWFORD, CORNWALL

A BASKET OF flowers bumped Ben's leg as his footsteps crunched the shelled garden path. He shifted the handle to his other hand and hoped none of his brothers caught him in such compromising circumstances, else he'd never hear an end to their rudeness. Kate smiled as she set another perfectly formed rose atop her already prodigious pile, and his concerns faded.

"I shall never be half as accomplished at gardening as you, Kate." This was from Bronwyn, who walked with them, along with Kate's young sister Alys.

"What nonsense," Kate said, laughing. "We live in Cornwall, where flowers sprout from rocks.

Anyone can grow them."

"Wildflowers, yes, but I doubt anyone has your talent for roses."

"Pish," Kate said with a wave of one gloved hand. She'd understated her talents again, as she often did. They walked among the gardens of the Parker home, where elegant roses with their warm fragrance stood in silent disapproval of their poor relations—the wildflowers—growing with abandon beyond the wall. A glasshouse stood some distance from the main house, where Kate's father tended his specimens, but the roses, Ben knew, were all Kate's doing.

Alys turned to him and begged, "Tell us again of London." Kate's sister was not one given to restraint. Her eyes sparkled as she idly smoothed her fingers along the satin hair ribbons he'd brought from his travels.

"Ben has already obliged you twice," Kate said, though not unkindly.

"But I'd like to hear his stories again. There's nothing so grand in Newford as a London ball. I should like to have all the delicious details."

"I suspect my cousin has kept some of the delicious details to himself," Bronwyn muttered.

"Oh!" Alys said as she came to a full stop. "Do you have stories that are *inappropriate for delicate ears*?"

"Alys!" Kate said as Ben chuckled. It hadn't

escaped him that his friends and family—all of Newford, in fact—assumed his visits to London were spent in idle, debauched amusement.

"If I had such stories, Mouse, d'you think I'd share them with you?"

"Well, you should," she argued as she kicked at a stone in the path. "How else am I to prepare for the rakes and rogues and scoundrels?"

"What d'you know of such things?" Ben asked with a frown.

"Precisely nothing, and that's the point. Papa has promised I'm to have a season, but I can't go to London in ignorance."

Ben adopted a serious tone. "But you can't be more than twelve. To be sure, a season must be ages away yet."

Predictably, Alys gasped at this affront to her dignity. "I'm nearly fifteen and will have my season in two years. Surely Kate will be married by *then*."

Ben slid a glance toward Kate in time to see the merest blush appear on her cheeks. Clearing his throat, he said with a smile, "Then I will leave it to your Papa to educate you on the perils of London."

"Oh, very well. But you didn't used to be such a stuffed shirt."

Bronwyn laughed. "Nicely said," she murmured as she looped an arm through Alys's. The pair walked ahead, and Ben heard her add, "I think it must be the first complaint of that sort my cousin has ever had."

Their voices and steps faded as they moved down the shell path, and a warm breeze brought salt from the sea to mingle with the intoxicating fragrance of Kate's blooms.

"Thank you again for the gloves," she said as she explored the soft kid leather. "They're lovely."

He'd thought of Kate and her roses as soon as he'd seen the garden gloves in a shop window on Oxford Street. He only wished he hadn't found her in the roses today, already gloved, so he might see them on her. She replaced the lid on the box and settled it in the basket.

"I made a guess at the size," he said. "I hope they're a good fit."

"Oh, they're perfect. I'm certain of it."

Ben waited with the basket as she leaned forward to snip another stem, turning his attention to the valley that rolled and stretched below. It was crossed with low, bramble-covered hedges that formed a poorly stitched quilt thrown across the green landscape. And standing sentry above the whole, not far from where they stood, was a small stone structure.

He released a silent sigh for the aptly named Kimbrell's Folly. The miniature castle, complete with crenelated battlements and a crumbling tower, held fast to the hillside. It was too much to expect the thing would have tumbled to the sea by now, or that the trees would have grown to hide his foolishness, but at least the ivy and wild roses had begun their assault. Perhaps in another decade or three, all of Newford would forget its existence.

"Your father has promised Alys a season?" he asked. It was as much an effort to gauge Kate's thoughts as to distract his own.

She nodded, though she didn't look up from her task. "In London, no less," she said.

"D'you think he'll remember when the time comes?"

"No." A sigh accompanied this. "But as Alys says, perhaps I'll be married by then, and *I* can give her a season."

Ben smiled, but it felt tilty, as if his lips wouldn't quite curve up on both sides.

Kate placed another stem atop his basket, a pale pink bud still damp with the morning's dew. "There," she said. "These ought to brighten Mr. Simmons' table." She turned to face him more fully, and he saw a black-speckled ladybird had landed at the top of her sleeve.

"Hold a moment," he said as he shifted the basket to his other hand. She stilled and waited as he lifted a finger to the soft muslin of her gown. Ben realized then how close they stood. Inappropriately close. Close enough that he could see himself reflected in her dark eyes. The air between them shifted and warmed, and birds stilled in the trees. He wondered if Kate felt it too.

He thought of the bonfire they'd enjoyed so many springs before. Of his failed kiss and Kate's unfinished question. She'd been unable to voice the words, and he still didn't know if she'd been relieved or disappointed at his answer. Since then, he'd devised a few—or rather, an entire deck's worth—of witty responses he might have offered instead. *Anything* would have been better than what he'd given her.

He might have surprised her with a confession: *Common rogue? I'm as common as they come. D'you think I'll scruple over a bit of thievery?*

Or he could have confounded her with a heartfelt plea: *Save me from the gallows, Kate, for a kiss freely given can't be stolen.* He nearly snorted aloud at that one, but Kate was not a lady to be trifled with. She was his friend and, if not a princess in fact, then near enough to one. A kiss between them would change everything.

Always, he wondered what her reply might have been if he'd simply offered her the truth that first spring. But that had been his perfectly imperfect spring, when so many things were right and so many were wrong. And whenever he thought on what he'd hoped to gain back then, he recalled all he'd lost instead.

Kate watched him, bemused, so he turned his hand for her to see the tiny beetle he'd collected from her sleeve.

"A ladybird!" she said as they watched it fly away. "Oh, you're in for a spell of good fortune."

"'Twas you she settled upon. I believe the fortune to be had is yours."

"Perhaps we'll both experience a happy change in our fates."

"How very un-Christian of you," he said with a smile, "to believe in equal happiness for all."

"How very Byron of you," she retorted, "to speak with such irony."

"Would that be... 'Byrony'? Kate, I believe you've coined a new word. We should alert someone."

Eyeing him sideways, she said, "You are ridiculous, you know."

Free hand to his chest, he assured her, "'Tis a cross, but someone must bear't."

She shook her head and continued along the path, but she was smiling. He followed. Then, clearing his throat, he motioned to the basket to say, "Why d'you bother with flowers for old Mr. Simmons? To be sure, he'll not appreciate them as he ought."

"With his sons gone and now that his wife has passed, his home seems... I don't know. Tired, perhaps. Although, I suppose that's a silly thing to say—a home isn't like a person, to appear tired and weary."

Ben considered her words for the length of three paces. "I disagree," he said. "Buildings take on the souls of their inhabitants, so 'tis a perfectly reasonable observation."

Kate considered this rare bit of seriousness falling from his lips. "Do you know," she said. "I think you're right. Ridiculous or not, you've always had a keen intuition." His neck warmed beneath her regard until she angled her head at him in amusement.

"What?" he whispered. "D'you also wonder if I've returned with tales inappropriate for delicate ears?"

She laughed. "I've no need to speculate on that point, as I'm certain you must have. No, I was simply struck by the image you make, standing there with my basket of flowers. I can only imagine what your brothers would say."

"'Tis probably best if we don't tell them."

"Your secret is safe with me," she assured him. Then, indicating Bronwyn some paces ahead, she added, "I can't offer any promises, though, regarding your cousin's discretion."

He dipped his head in rueful acknowledgement, but the truth of it was, an hour strolling amongst the flowers with Kate was worth any rudeness he might suffer later.

CHAPTER TWO

KATE TUGGED AT the fingertips of her gloves, but she didn't remove them, no matter how she itched to bury her fingers in the damp soil at their feet. But her grandmother and namesake — the formidable Lady Catherine Dunne — would have her believe gardening without gloves simply wasn't the thing, so she stilled her hands and clasped them behind her.

It was her favorite time of year, when the cliffs and hedgerows, meadows and moors, came alive in a brief accord. When the honeyed scent of blooming gorse mingled with sea salt, and the bluebells, foxgloves, and wild garlic embroidered the brown landscape of winter. There was nothing like spring in Cornwall.

And, as if the burgeoning season weren't enough to lift her spirits, Ben had finally returned from

London. She still wished to take him to task for hying off without so much as a by-your-leave, but she'd grown accustomed to his comings and goings. Every few months, he'd take himself off to London for a spell, leaving her to wonder what amusements he was getting up to and if he thought of his friends back in Newford. But she'd set aside her irritation and for now, she simply took an easy breath, drawing in the pleasure of the day and the sun's warming rays.

"Alfie seems to have settled well into his marriage," she said as she checked the closed buds of a striped cabbage rose. Ben's brother, who only months before had been one of Newford's staunchest bachelors, had recently married a lady writer from Truro. By all appearances, the two were well matched.

Ben nodded, tipping her one of his delightfully crooked grins. "Aye. Miss Darling—Eliza, rather—suits him, despite their disparities in temperament. I don't hesitate to tell you though—my brother has become insufferable in his newfound knowledge of the marriage state."

Kate lifted a silent brow in inquiry.

"Aye, 'tis true. He tried to advise Wynne and Roddie on the finer points of marital discourse and nearly lost a finger for his efforts."

"A finger!"

"Wynne was helping Peggy in the kitchen at the time. 'Twasn't my brother's keenest moment."

Kate laughed. Ben was irreverent, as always, but the light in his eyes suggested he was well aware of the fact. She turned the subject, a smile still in her voice. "We've had a number of lady visitors since you've been away to London. It seems Miss Darling's Inventory has been quite the success."

She referred to Eliza's recent publication on Newford's eligible bachelors, whose numbers far outpaced the eligible ladies. The article had become known simply as the Newford Inventory, and its result had been a shocking influx of visitors to their small hamlet.

Ben shifted the basket to his other hand to guide her around a puddle. "I understand the second printing sold out in a matter of hours," he said. "I even heard a pair of ladies in Bath nearly came to blows over their bookseller's last copy."

"Truly?" Kate pulled her head back in disbelief.

"You doubt that Newford's bachelors can inspire such fervor?" His words and tone were serious, but a playful smile lurked in his eyes.

"I doubt you can resist teasing me, even if it requires gilding the facts a bit."

He laughed, neither confirming nor denying her charge.

With a press of her lips for his teasing, Kate said,

"And your cousins… what do they think of the Newford Inventory?"

"To be sure, they make a bit of noise over the attention it's received, but I suspect they're rather intrigued by it all."

Intrigued. Kate checked the frown that tugged at her brow, but it wouldn't do if Newford's gentlemen became too intrigued with the marriage-minded ladies pursuing the town's bachelors. She'd lately come to the inevitable conclusion that she must take steps if she meant to marry. Though she'd had suitors during her seasons in Bath, none had sufficiently tempted her. But time marched on regardless and so, after rigorous consideration and consultation with Bronwyn, she'd placed her friend's brother at the top of her list of prospective husbands.

Kate had shared a few dances and some conversation with Merryn Kimbrell. Each experience had been pleasant enough. Certainly, they'd not been *un*pleasant, and she'd begun to hope that, with a bit of encouragement, he might come to feel the same.

Marriage to Merryn Kimbrell was not without its benefits. Not only would she gain Bronwyn as a sister, but Merryn had a promising future leading his family's building firm. He was handsome and respectable. Kind, steadfast and earnest. He was not the sort of impulsive gentleman to hie himself off to London without telling a person.

But with flocks of marriage-minded ladies arriving to acquaint themselves with Newford's eligible gentlemen, she'd do well to engage Merryn's interest before too much time had passed. With an inward sigh, Kate shoved the thought to the back of her mind and returned her attention to Ben.

"I understand *you* didn't contribute to Miss Darling's article," she said. "Has something changed—perhaps a lady somewhere has finally captured your notice?"

He slowed his step, and the basket swayed in his grip. "No," he said. "Nothing has changed."

The color in his cheeks was a little higher, and Kate studied him more closely. When his gaze slid from hers, she chewed her lip. She'd been teasing him—turnabout was fair, after all—but *had* Ben developed an affection for someone? Was that the reason for his trips to London?

Her chest tightened at the thought, but though she tried, she couldn't make the scenario fit. Ben had never been serious enough to fix his interest on any one lady. He might flirt with them, but he wasn't the sort to marry. Marriage and children required a dependable and steady nature. And Ben, though she loved him dearly, was not the sort to remember to pay the grocer's bill.

But what else but romance could account for the sudden color in his cheeks? The sun, which had been spring-bright earlier, seemed to dim a little.

Bronwyn and Alys, having reached the end of the garden path, returned to them with sure steps. "We should hurry, Kate," Bronwyn said, "or we'll miss tea with the Ladies' Society. If we don't cast our votes, you know we'll be obliged to perform some dreadful but improving play instead of something fun."

Kate called up a smile, wishing she'd not agreed to attend the Ladies' Society meeting. She had no intention of performing—the very thought of taking the stage caused no little anxiety to dampen her palms—and she'd much rather be checking the roses for pests anyway.

"Let me just return my things to the glasshouse," she said with resignation as she untied her apron.

"What are Newford's esteemed ladies getting up to now?" Ben asked.

"Now that we've a theater, it's occurred to some—"

"Rather belatedly," Bronwyn interjected.

"—*rather belatedly*, that perhaps we ought to organize a performance. Given all of our new visitors, we don't wish to be seen as provincial, you understand."

"But we are provincial."

Kate smiled and whispered in an aside, "Don't tell that to Mrs. Clifton." Taking her basket from him, she added, "Thank you for playing footman."

"I stand ready to serve," he returned with a bold wink.

She lifted her brows at that bit of nonsense.

"Too brown?" he said.

"Too brown. But I can't argue that you're the dearest of friends, and I'm so pleased you've returned."

———

KATE ENTERED THEIR delightfully humid glasshouse and returned her apron to its peg. Her father stood at a low cabinet in the far corner, head down as he sorted seeds into bins. She joined him and set her basket aside to remove her soiled gardening gloves.

"I'm away, Papa," she said. "Bronwyn and I are joining the Ladies' Society for tea."

A moment passed before he looked up and another after that before his gaze cleared. "What's that?"

"The Ladies' Society meeting. It's today."

"Oh, yes. Yes, of course. Does Edith Pentreath still run roughshod over everyone?"

"Papa," she scolded softly before relenting with a twist of her lips. "Perhaps a bit."

He turned back to his seeds, but his gaze caught on the flat box atop her basket. "You've another fancy box from London. Ben Kimbrell has returned, I take it?"

Kate pulled her head back in surprise that her parent, whose thoughts were more often on his botanical children than his human ones, would notice such a thing. "Gloves," she confirmed as she lifted the lid. "Aren't they lovely?" They were almost too beautiful to risk soiling.

Her father removed his spectacles to rub his eyes. "In my day, gloves were tantamount to a proposal."

Kate laughed. "A proposal? From Ben Kimbrell?" The words felt unnatural. "I think your new fertilizer has addled your brain, Papa."

"Hmm," was his only response. She stretched to kiss his cheek. As she reached the door to go, he called out. "I almost forgot. Lady Catherine is coming for an Extended Visit." He spoke the last words with extra emphasis and a touch of foreboding.

Kate's stomach dipped in reflex. "Grandmother's coming? When?"

"I had a letter from her just last week... or was it two weeks ago?" He rubbed his spectacles with a cloth, and his whiskered cheeks puffed as he searched his memory. "At any rate, I imagine she'll descend—er, arrive—sooner than either of us would like."

Kate nodded, but her thoughts had already turned to a critical assessment of the dining room and parlor. Though spotless already, the public rooms wouldn't be any worse for another dusting, and the silver could use a good polish. Her grandmother's visits weren't frequent, but they were memorable, if only for the anxiety they produced amongst family and servants alike.

Once the Ladies' Society meeting was ended, she'd see that her grandmother's room was readied. Lady Catherine would bring her own maids—two of them—so that was something, at least. But the rugs should be beaten and meals must be planned. Three courses, at least, though more would be expected. The daughter of a marquess wouldn't suffer informal fare.

CHAPTER THREE

BEN RETRIEVED HIS horse from the Parkers' groom and took the winding lane down the hill to Newford. He'd promised his cousin he'd assist with roof repairs at the inn's stables, and he'd spent more time than he ought to have toting flowers about. Gravel spun beneath the horse's hooves as he descended the final turn, and the market clock chimed the hour. He slowed the horse to a walk and reached the yard of the Fin and Feather Inn as the Bath stage was leaving.

With a toss of the reins to the inn's ostler, he entered the cool stone building. Recent spring storms had taken their toll on Newford's rooftops, and Merryn stood with a pair of his men, pointing out several new spots of daylight visible in the tall ceiling. He glanced up at Ben's entrance and gave an impatient tap of his hat against his thigh, but he didn't interrupt his instruction.

Finally, Merryn dismissed the men with a nod and turned his attention to Ben. "You're late, Cousin."

"Apologies. I was detained." At the skeptical lift of his cousin's brow, Ben added, "'Twas unavoidable."

"Aye, 'tis always the way."

Ben had no response to that, so he listened as his cousin explained what needed to be done on the roof, then he turned to go.

"Ben," Merryn called before he could clear the door.

"Aye?" Ben didn't turn but listened for whatever wisdom or rebuke his cousin might offer.

"Did your weeks in London meet your expectations?"

The question wasn't what he'd anticipated, although he should have. "Aye." The word was reluctant.

A long beat passed before Merryn replied. "Then why, for all that's holy, have you come to do slate work?"

"'Tis good work."

Merryn's sigh, when it came, was so soft he almost didn't hear it. Then, an afterthought from Merryn as Ben continued toward the sunlit inn yard: "Don't forget your rope!"

His cousin was a stickler. No one but Merryn required the use of a rope. Although tempted to ignore the reminder, Ben wasn't such a fool as that. He'd not risk his neck for the sole, though satisfying, pleasure of annoying Merryn, so he collected his rope before eyeing the ladder propped against the stone wall.

The Feather's stables were three stories tall with an oversized ground floor to accommodate the large London mail coaches, a first-floor hayloft and grooms' quarters on the second. Only the ancient parish church with its sturdy Norman tower could boast a higher prospect. The stables' roof was steeply pitched, each course of slate blending seamlessly with the one beneath it, the whole accented by a band of scallop-edged tiles.

Dragging in a measured breath, Ben placed his boot on the first rung, then the next. The ladder wobbled beneath his weight, but it didn't set his heart to pounding. Ladders were never the problem. Heights were never the problem. That would come later, when he took his feet off the rungs to stand on the tiles.

He climbed, steadily ascending until he reached the top. Then, sweat dampening his palms and unease knotting his belly, he stepped onto the slate and slowly looked up. The village stretched before him, the small harbor to one end and the church with its bell tower at the other.

Mrs. Pentreath walked along the high street, her cane thumping the pavers and a cap pinned to her steel grey curls. A pair of ladies passed her as they left their lodgings at the Feather arm in arm. He could hear their low giggles as they navigated the cobbles. Some of the Newford Inventory arrivals, he presumed, on the hunt for bachelors.

The day was a clear one with views stretching to the middle of the sea. The combined scents of spring and sea and something simmering in the Feather's kitchen would have filled him with optimism if they didn't cause such a familiar ache in his chest. In fact, the entire scene was much as it had been more than a decade before.

His mother hadn't been gone a fortnight yet, but he'd welcomed—no, he'd *needed*—the distraction of assisting his uncle on the roof. The day had been clear, the slates slick from the night's rain. The peace of working together in silence, high above the other rooftops, should have eased his sore heart. But that day, Ben left his tool where it oughtn't have been, and Pedrek Kimbrell—Merryn's father—had the misfortune of stepping on it.

Ben heard the unchecked slide of boots on slate and turned in time to see his uncle stop his fall with a wrenching grasp of the cast iron gutter. He rushed to his uncle's aid, but at thirteen, he'd been unable to lift him back to safety. He struggled in horror, fists tight about his uncle's wrists and tears blurring his vision as Pedrek's fingers slipped one by one from the gutter's edge. Help, when it came, had been too late. Night fell before anyone realized Ben remained atop the stables, knees to his chest, hands over his ears in a futile effort to block the sounds that wouldn't ease.

Now, nausea turned Ben's stomach. He pulled and released a slow breath to banish the images as he steadied himself.

Slate work. Of all the jobs his cousin might have had for him, why did it have to be slate work? If Merryn were a vengeful sort of man, Ben imagined he might have put him on rooftops for the sheer enjoyment of it, but his cousin's temperament was, by and large, an easy one.

Several baskets of slate had already been drawn up, and Merryn's men were deftly removing and resetting tiles. One looked up and waved his hammer, and Ben nodded in reply. Another wave of nausea tightened his stomach, and he forced it down before picking his way across the slates to loop his rope about the chimney.

"Ben!" Mr. Dickey called when Ben was within hailing distance. "Ye're returned from London."

"Aye." He tried to watch his step without appearing like he was watching his step.

"Did ye see the new king?"

"I saw him, though there's little different from when we knew him as Prinny. A bit more pomp to the procession, if 'tis possible."

"I imagine ye stayed up 'til all hours doing all manner o' things," Mr. Cole said.

All manner of things? What, precisely, did Newford think he got up to in London? "I attended the theater once or twice," Ben admitted.

From this perspective, with a clear view of the hills above Newford, he could just make out the pointed roof of Kimbrell's Folly beneath its green shroud of ivy. Dickey followed his gaze and chortled. "Still 'aven't finished it, 'ave ye? Let's 'ope ye've a better eye on today's task than ye did yer pretty folly."

Ben pressed his lips against a growl and pointed to a section of roof. "Shall I begin here then, lads?"

"Aye," Cole replied. "'Tis as good a place as any."

Ben pulled his claw hammer and set to work. The sun warmed his back as he carefully removed the damaged tiles. He took care not to disturb the surrounding slate, gently prying each piece up and easing it from under the tiles above it. Once he'd removed the damaged tiles, he inspected the wooden structure beneath for rot. Satisfied that the timbers didn't need replacing, he prepared new slates to fit the space and secured them with copper nails.

The process was tedious, but strangely satisfying. An odd sort of penance, but there it was. And he'd meant what he told his cousin; it *was* good work. Once he conquered his nerves, rather.

Slate work didn't have the same appeal as design work, though, nor did it require the same intensity of thought. In fact, little thought was required once he started, as his hands readily took over. But despite the nauseating reminders of past mistakes, slate work had one distinct advantage over anything else he might have done: certainly, he couldn't fail at it any more than he'd done already.

———

MERRYN STOOD AT the base of the ladder and shook his head slowly as his cousin navigated the Feather's steeply pitched roof. For someone with little direction to his life, Ben was one of the most stubborn people he knew. And he was a Kimbrell, so that was no small matter.

Ben's aversion to rooftops was a poorly kept secret. In fact, Ben was the only one who still thought it a secret at all, but anyone watching his measured steps above the Feather's stables could easily guess what the act cost him.

And it didn't require a tremendous effort to deduce the source of his unease. Merryn had been abed with a fever the day his father died, but he imagined the event must have left a mark on his cousin. No amount of careful probing over the years had loosened Ben's lips on the matter, though. Ben had kept his own counsel, locking his thoughts tight behind an easy grin.

Merryn had even gone so far as to discuss the matter with Dr. Rowe—discreetly, of course, and in the most general of terms. The good surgeon, though skilled at setting broken bones, had seemed at a loss to restore a broken spirit. "The best cure for your friend," he'd said with a skeptical glance above the rim of his spectacles, "is to confront the source of his disquiet."

Thus, the rooftop. Merryn had hoped putting his cousin on rooftops might fix whatever ailed him. At the very least, he'd thought it might motivate him to find his path again, one that utilized his natural talents more fully and with less peril. Clearly, he'd been mistaken on both counts.

Ben's brother Alfie joined him, shading his eyes against the white afternoon sun. "He's doing slate work again?"

"Aye."

Alfie frowned, adding slowly, "He's a talent for't, I suppose, despite his affliction."

Merryn's jaw tightened as he crossed his arms. "Your brother could be good at any number of things, many of which would not place his life in peril. But I know better than most that a Kimbrell's life is an easier thing to risk than his pride."

His brows came together as the words left his mouth. It occurred to him then that he'd not accounted for the rather predictable effect of a man's pride. *Ben's* pride, to be precise. He'd been going about things the wrong way.

No, something else must be done.

CHAPTER FOUR

THE NEWFORD LADIES' Society meeting was held in the Feather's upper rooms, as it had been for the past five years and more. While the ladies would argue over many things, no one disputed that innkeeper Wynne Teague laid a fine tea.

The room was spacious with high ceilings and floorboards that gleamed with wood polish. At the first of every month, they were dulled with chalk for Newford's assembly, and the large windows would be thrown open to cool overheated dancers. For today's purpose, though, neat rows of wooden-backed chairs lined the space, and a table laden with refreshments beckoned from a sheltered alcove at the back.

Morwenna Williams, another Kimbrell cousin, approached Kate and Bronwyn with a plate piled with cakes and raspberry tarts. She took the seat beside them then murmured around a mouthful of sponge cake, "I have it from Wynne that Mrs. P means to put an end to the play before it's even begun."

"But that's absurd," Bronwyn said. She lowered her voice to add, "What is the purpose of our new theater if we're never to present a play?"

Morwenna lifted a brow in silent agreement as she brushed a crumb from her skirts.

"Kate," Bronwyn said, "you must make her see reason."

"I? What sway can I have?"

"Your manners are unimpeachable," Bronwyn said. "Mrs. P thinks all of us Kimbrells are hoydenish, but she can't find fault with your perfection."

Kate would have frowned at that—she was certain there must have been an insult in there somewhere—but as Bronwyn pointed out, her manners were unimpeachable. So, instead, she remained silent and sipped her tea.

Presently, Edith Pentreath thumped her cane twice on the wood floor to begin the meeting, and there was a general shuffling as everyone found their seats. "Ladies," she began, "it's not enough that Newford suffers *two* coaching inns, which serve all manner of persons with varying degrees of moral fortitude. But now, despite the benefit of my very sound counsel, our esteemed leaders test our fiber with a *theater*."

She pulled in a restorative breath and continued, "Regardless of the wisdom of such a course, the die has been cast, and it falls to us to make the best of it. Our purpose today is to reach an accord regarding which production shall be our first. Some of our neighbors"—she aimed a gimlet eye toward Mrs. Clifton—"believe a theater will be a boon, while others, myself included, have grave concerns. It is incumbent upon all of us to choose a production that reflects the values and high moral standards of Newford."

It didn't take long for the debate to fire up from there, with clear sides taken. Mrs. Clifton, whose husband owned the bakery and looked forward to an increase in custom, was in full support of a play that would *not* cast Newford in the role of provincial backwater.

"Edith," Mrs. Clifton said, "Truro's theater has a long history of cultural sophistication, and I know our mayor would not like Newford to show to disadvantage."

"Truro is hardly a suitable measuring stick."

"What do we know of putting on a proper production?" Mrs. Tretheway said. Wherever Mrs. Pentreath went, Mrs. Tretheway followed. "To be sure, there will be expenses to consider, and we don't have the experience to match the larger villages. We don't know the first thing about costumes and sets and the like."

Mrs. Clifton's bosom puffed with import. "I attended a play in Truro some years back, Charlotte, and I've a fair notion of how it's done."

"That was *ten* years agone, Agnes."

For any argument Mrs. Clifton made, Mrs. Pentreath was equally adamant that any production was sure to invite sin, and she claimed to have the vicar on her side.

"But surely, there can be no disagreement with Shakespeare," Bronwyn offered. "All the Bard's best plays are done in London."

Mrs. Pentreath's cap quivered. "Just because they are done in London, Miss Kimbrell, does not mean they should be done here. I would not expect you to know anything of it, but Mr. Shakespeare's plays can be quite inappropriate. There is often kissing, and the language!"

Mrs. Tretheway followed this with, "To be sure, a Shakespearean play is too fast for our humble hamlet!"

"On the contrary, ma'am," Morwenna said, "While 'tis true his plays can be controversial, they provide innumerable opportunities for moral instruction. Just think of the lessons we could impart in the virtues of duty and humility."

From the corner of her eye, Kate saw Bronwyn give her cousin a congratulatory nudge. She fought a smile until Bronwyn's other elbow connected with her own rib. "What are your thoughts, Miss Parker?"

"My thoughts?" Truthfully, as long as she wasn't required to perform, she wasn't overly particular. But they awaited her response, so she said, "I... I suppose we might select one of Mr. Shakespeare's less objectionable plays and... donate the proceeds to the children's home. Surely that's a compromise neither our mayor nor our vicar can find fault with."

"Nicely done," Bronwyn whispered.

After further debate followed by more quivering of Mrs. Pentreath's cap, it was finally decided. The Ladies' Society would present *Much Ado About Nothing* in one month's time, and the proceeds would benefit the poor, unfortunate souls at the parish home.

"Miss Parker, I think you shall play the female lead," Mrs. Pentreath declared. "Betsy or Blanche, I believe—"

"Oh, but—"

"It's Beatrice, ma'am," Bronwyn volunteered. "The female lead, that is."

"Beatrice then," Mrs. Pentreath acknowledged with a tightening of her lips.

"But—" Kate tried again.

"My cousin Ben can play Benedick," Bronwyn said, and Mrs. Pentreath's lips nearly disappeared altogether. "They do share a name, after all,"

Bronwyn added in a reasonable, if slightly defensive, tone.

Kate cast a skeptical glance at her friend. She didn't think Ben would thank his cousin for offering him up, just as Kate had no desire to play Beatrice. "Mrs. Pentreath," she said, lifting her voice so she might be heard. "I'm certain there must be someone better suited to the role of Beatrice. Perhaps I could assist with the costumes instead."

"I'll rest easier knowing the lead is in your sensible hands, Miss Parker."

Kate imagined a theater full of people, all eyes on her as she played the part of Beatrice. Talking to one person—or a small group, even—posed no problem. But the thought of *performing*...

And then there was Lady Catherine to consider. Her grandmother would not approve any relation of hers treading the boards. Kate's stomach took an uncomfortable turn, and she pressed a hand against her middle. Straightening, she cleared her throat. "I'm not unaware of the honor, ma'am, but if it's all the same, I'd rather not."

The room went silent at this declaration—an unusual bit of boldness coming from the demure Miss Parker—and her cheeks warmed. Bronwyn leaned close to whisper, "Ben will play Benedick. Are you certain you don't wish to play Beatrice?"

Kate stared at her friend in confusion. "I—I'm

certain," she said, assuring her with her eyes that she'd never been more so. Then, in an aside, she added, "Lady Catherine is coming for A Visit."

Bronwyn's eyes widened in understanding. With a nod, she said to Mrs. Pentreath, "I played Beatrice in a small production we organized as children. Though I agree Miss Parker would make a splendid Beatrice, I'd be happy to take up the role again if she has other commitments."

Mrs. Pentreath eyed the three of them, lips pursed as if her raspberry tart had gone off. "Miss Kimbrell," she said, "this is a serious business. We'll not have any mischief."

"Upon my honor, ma'am." Bronwyn solemnized this oath with an irreverent two-fingered cross of her heart.

"Hmm." Mrs. Pentreath had the knowledge of more than six decades of the Kimbrell clan. Her own sister's head had been turned by a dashing member of the family during the height of their smuggling days. That the Kimbrells had been as straight as a kingfisher's beak for nearly twenty years mattered not a whit in her book.

Finally, with an audible sigh, she relented. "Very well then," she said before returning her attention to Kate. "Miss Parker, I'll trust you to see that this production maintains all due propriety."

"Yes, ma'am." Kate replied.

CHAPTER FIVE

B EN, HAVING FINISHED the day's tribulation, emerged from the Feather's stables to be met by Kate and Bronwyn. Their meeting of the Ladies' Society was concluded, and he left his horse behind so he might escort them to their homes. Bronwyn prattled on about the ladies' vote, which he understood had been "a near thing," as they walked along the lane above Newford.

Some moments later, he realized with a start that his attention had wandered to the faint rose scent of Kate's hair. When he heard his name and the phrase "dramatic performance," he forced himself to attend the conversation.

"What production did the ladies agree upon?" he asked. "And more importantly, how does it concern me?"

"Oh, it will be great fun," Bronwyn assured him,

which was to say he wouldn't like it very much.

"Bronwyn..."

"You will play Benedick—"

"I will what?"

"And I will play Beatrice. It will be the best production of *Much Ado About Nothing* that Cornwall—that *England*—has ever seen. Though, to be honest, I'm a bit staggered that Mrs. P didn't kick up more of a fuss over your involvement."

She said this last with enough surprise to give offense, but he brushed that off to say, "And how, precisely, did I come to be cast in a role for this?"

"Well, who else could do justice to Benedick's witty banter with the lovely Beatrice? And your name, of course, makes you a natural fit"—he frowned at that poor logic—"although I believe Mrs. P prefers Kate's good sense over any Kimbrell performance."

Ben looked down at Kate. She shrugged and a charming blush spread across her fair cheeks. "Saint Kate?" he said. He couldn't disagree with Mrs. P, but he did enjoy watching Kate's color deepen.

She scowled. "There is nothing wrong with having a reputation which others admire. And besides," she added with a narrowing of her eyes, "you can't argue that someone must keep the Kimbrells in check."

He pressed a hand to his heart. "I can think of no

one better suited. Per'aps this won't be such a dreadful ordeal after all, if you're there to stand as our compass." Lifting her hand, he dropped an exaggerated kiss on her knuckles through the thin cotton of her glove.

She pulled her hand from his in exasperation, but she was smiling. Her smile quickly fell, though, when the urgent clattering of swiftly turning wheels sounded beyond a bend in the lane ahead. Some fool was taking the hill too fast and—

High screams rose on the air, but all came to an abrupt stop with a resounding crash that sent birds fleeing from the hedges. Ben stood motionless for a single heartbeat before he raced forward, Kate and Bronwyn close behind.

They rounded the curve to find a once elegant carriage on its side at the bottom of the rise. The top-most wheels still turned in the air, and glass from the shattered windows reflected splintered sunlight from the ground. The hedgerows had gone silent without the birds' ever-present chatter, and the combined scents of newly turned earth and fresh beech sap hung in the air.

Ben rushed toward the equipage and peered down into the carriage. Two women huddled amidst scattered reticules and gloves, their faces stark with shock.

It was clear to see the driver had taken the curve

too fast, but he was nowhere to be seen and had probably been thrown clear of the vehicle. The horses, having come free of their harnesses, circled uneasily, eyes wide and nostrils flaring. Bronwyn approached them slowly in an attempt to soothe their disquiet as Kate searched for the driver beyond the dense undergrowth at the lane's edge.

"Ladies," Ben said into the carriage, "we'll have you out of there in a trice. Is anyone injured?"

"N—no," a tremulous voice said. "I don't think so. We've a few bumps but nothing too grievous."

Ben introduced himself to set them at their ease.

"Yes, yes, of course," the tremulous lady said as she straightened. She wore an elegant widow's gown of grey silk and an askew lavender bonnet trimmed with a broken feather. "I'm Mrs. Matthews, newly arrived from London," she said as Ben began working the latch on the door. "And this is my companion, Miss Whittlesby."

Ben nodded to each of them in turn. As far as introductions went, this had to be one of the more memorable ones he'd ever experienced. The latch wasn't giving so he adjusted his hold on the wood and pulled again.

"And are you come to visit acquaintances in Newford?" he asked.

"No," Mrs. Matthews said. "That is, we've merely come to take in the sights."

Ah. Newford had few sights worth taking in, and certainly not for those accustomed to London's attractions. He could only assume the young widow was another of the marriage-minded ladies who'd come to shop for a husband among the town's bachelors. His suspicion was confirmed when he spotted a bent copy of the Newford Inventory among their things at the bottom of the carriage.

Bronwyn and Kate, having found the driver, tended a small cut on the man's forehead a short distance from the wreckage. Hooves sounded on the lane behind them and Ben turned as Merryn rode up. His cousin jumped from his horse and cast the driver an assessing glance before striding toward Ben and the carriage.

"Is anyone else hurt?" he asked.

"Merely a few bumps. The door, though—'tis a bit stubborn." Ben kept his words soft and even so as not to alarm the ladies.

Merryn nodded and peered into the carriage. "Ladies, we'll have you out of there in a trice."

Ben resisted the urge to roll his eyes and braced himself on one side of the door as Merryn stepped into position on the other. They gripped the frame tightly and pulled, straining against the thick mahogany. The door groaned, but the latch held fast, refusing to release its grip.

Merryn muttered an oath under his breath, and

Ben shared the sentiment. He stood with his hands on his hips, searching the wreckage for inspiration. Spotting a jagged piece of wood nearby, he lifted it, testing the weight in his hand. "I've an idea…" His gaze shifted to the door's hinges. "We can't get the door off from this angle, but let's see if we can't break the hinges instead."

Merryn nodded. "'Tis worth a try."

Positioning themselves once more, Ben wedged the wood between the door and frame and pressed firmly. Merryn followed suit, adding his own strength to the endeavor. With each exertion, the hinges creaked and protested, but the door remained obstinate. Sweat dotted Ben's brow, and blood ran from a cut on his hand as they gave one more heave against the wood. Finally, there was a satisfying crack, and the door gave way.

"Oh, you've saved us!" A breathy voice said from inside the carriage. He thought it might have been Miss Whittlesby, but he couldn't be certain. He lifted the door and tossed it aside as Merryn extended a hand into the carriage. Mrs. Matthews came first, leaning heavily against Merryn and favoring one ankle as she stepped to the ground.

Merryn led her to a low stump as Ben assisted Miss Whittlesby away from the wreckage. Once he was confident the ladies were secure, he took a moment to wrap the cut on his hand. As he did so,

Kate approached. He grinned, inordinately pleased with the day's success, but she continued walking until she reached Merryn's side. Ben's grin turned to a frown of confusion. He might have been a field mouse perched on the nearby hedge for all the notice Kate spared him.

She extended a linen square for Merryn, who smiled as he took it. The two of them exchanged whispered words, and Ben's stomach tightened. His cousin sported a tiny cut on his palm—Ben could barely see it from where he stood, so small was the injury—but Kate's brow puckered in dismay as if he'd suffered a mortal wound. What was this about?

Motion to his left caught his attention, and he turned to find Bronwyn had joined him. She squeezed his hand, applying stout pressure to his own cut beneath his handkerchief, and he winced. Head down, she muttered something that sounded like, "Gawky idiot."

He wasn't sure whom, precisely, had earned her disapproval, but he couldn't disagree with the sentiment.

———

RELIEVED TO FIND the carriage's occupants largely unscathed, Kate turned her thoughts to less urgent matters. She'd had the foresight to tuck her best linen square into her reticule that morning, and now she extended it to Merryn. "For your injury," she said.

He returned her smile with an easy one of his own. "Your concern is welcomed, Miss Parker, but hardly necessary. You can see I've escaped with little more than a scratch, and I wouldn't want to soil your handkerchief for such a minor injury."

"I insist," she said. How was she to secure Merryn's interest if he wouldn't even accept a dratted handkerchief?

To her relief, he took the square with another smile and a polite nod and pressed the cloth to his palm. She wondered if he might remark the quality of her stitching or the linen's pleasing fragrance. Only yesterday she'd prepared a new rose-scented sachet for her linen drawer. Or perhaps he'd comment on the softness of the cloth itself…. She watched and waited.

"The stitching is nicely done," he said obligingly. "Are these…?"

"They're bluebells," she replied with a smile.

"They're lovely. You've a fine hand."

"Thank you."

"I shall see it properly laundered and returned to you," he promised.

Kate licked her lips. *Tell him to keep it*, her mind urged. *Tell him!* But no matter her mind's urging, all she said was, "You'll want to be sure to clean the cut properly. If you've chamomile, your cook can prepare an infusion." *Truly? Chamomile infusions?*

"Sensible words from a sensible lass. Thank you."

"It's a small injury now, but you wouldn't want it to worsen." *Stop talking.*

"Of course," he said agreeably.

Kate drew a calming breath. What next? Her tongue seemed to fail her whenever it was called into service around Merryn. With some relief, she recalled the lady being tended by her companion nearby. Turning to them, she said, "I'm Miss Parker."

"Mrs. Matthews," the lady replied with a small nod before introducing her companion. Mrs. Matthews wore a nicely cut gown of pale grey silk beneath a fetching pelisse. A small jet mourning brooch indicated her widowed state. With pale skin Kate was certain could only be achieved with cosmetics, hair the color of old copper and eyes like a stormy Cornish sea, she was quite arresting.

"Your driver has suffered some bruises and a cut above his brow, but I believe he'll recover."

"That is a relief to hear," Miss Whittlesby said.

"Aye," Merryn agreed. "But 'twould appear Mrs. Matthews has turned her ankle. Can you stand on the foot?" he asked the lady.

"I believe so."

Merryn extended a hand to assist her. Mrs. Matthews rose and attempted to put weight on the limb but quickly stumbled. Merryn caught her gently against him, and Kate's eyes widened as he carefully assisted the widow back to her stump. Of course he would assist her—to do any less would make him a cad—but his manner seemed overly solicitous.

Mrs. Matthews laughed—a light, flirtatious sound like water rippling over sun-warmed stones. "I'm afraid I've underestimated the pain or overestimated my own tolerance for it."

"Newford is naught but a short and pleasant walk from here," Merryn said. "I've a horse that can take you down, and we'll send someone to right the carriage and collect your things. D'you stay at the Fin and Feather Inn?"

Mrs. Matthews gazed up at Merryn, and the broken feather in her bonnet bounced becomingly over one sea-blue eye. "Yes," she said. "Miss Whittlesby and I—we thank you for your assistance. We're only just arrived, and already Newford welcomes us with extraordinary kindness."

Kate checked her frown, certain the lady's corset strings must be too tight as her words had a slightly breathless quality to them. Merryn extended an arm, oblivious of the lady's respiratory issues as she settled a hand on his sleeve. Kate watched their retreating forms as he led the limping widow and her companion to his waiting horse.

"The Newford Inventory," Bronwyn muttered from Kate's side. "Will we never see an end to its madness?"

Kate startled, not having heard her friend's approach. "You think the lady has come seeking a husband?" She returned her gaze to the visitors, and her frown grew as Merryn assisted Mrs. Matthews over a rut in the lane. Sore ankle notwithstanding, the lady didn't have much spirit if she couldn't manage such a tiny dip in the path without assistance.

"I saw a copy of the Inventory at the bottom of their carriage. It appeared a bit frayed about the edges," Bronwyn said meaningfully.

"But she's a widow, and still in half-mourning by the looks of it," Kate said. "Surely, she's not in the market for a husband so soon."

Bronwyn shrugged. "Perhaps they've merely come to take in the sights, as they say, although she wouldn't be the first widow to seek the security of a new husband before her mourning is finished."

Kate swallowed. "Your brother hasn't shown any interest in the Inventory's readers," she said slowly. "Surely, there's no reason he would do so now."

Bronwyn eyed her for the length of two breaths. "Are you certain you—" She stopped and collected her words before finishing with, "You're right, of course." Her tone, encouraging but not quite believable, gave Kate pause.

If she couldn't secure Merryn's affections, the past weeks would have been for naught. She'd have to set her sights on someone else, and the thought of that was more than a trifle exhausting. She looked up to see Merryn leaning closer to Mrs. Matthews's drooping feather, and dismay tightened her chest.

CHAPTER SIX

KATE AND... MERRYN? Ben rubbed the side of his jaw and forced the muscles there to relax. Of course, Kate must marry someday. He was surprised she'd not done so before now. With three seasons in Bath behind her, she should have long since made a respectable match. She was well on her way to spinsterhood, but for three seasons, they'd made their good-byes, and three times she'd returned.

But after all this time, had she finally set her heart on someone? Had she and Merryn developed an affection for one another while he'd been away? He shook his head in disbelief—the notion was as implausible as it was absurd. As far as he knew, the pair of them had never looked twice at one another before, but he couldn't deny their heads had been tucked quite close as they'd conversed over her linen square. Had she given him one of her bluebell-embroidered bits?

He shook his head to clear it. Kate and Merryn. His mind couldn't reconcile the notion.

Merryn had gone ahead with Mrs. Matthews and her companion while Kate and Bronwyn continued along the lane to Kate's home. With slow feet, he and the coachman saw to the carriage horses, guiding them down the lane and ensuring they were well settled in the Feather's stables with two large buckets of oats. Ben prepared to turn his steps toward his own supper when his cousin hailed him from the Feather's entry.

"Ben," Merryn called. "A moment of your time?" Ben's reluctance must have shown, for Merryn added, "There's an ale in it for you."

Well. Every man must have his price.

Ben nodded once then ducked beneath the Feather's low lintel. He crossed the uneven slate floor to the large window table in the coffee room. Several of his cousins were already gathered round with mugs of ale and glasses of dark amber whisky. Snagging a chair with his foot, he dropped into it as Peggy, the inn's barmaid, slid another tankard across the table's polished surface.

"Ben, we're pleased you've returned to the fold," Jory said with a bone-jolting clap to his shoulder. "Have you come to share your most recent escapades in London?"

Jory's collie, Trout, lifted her head from Jory's foot. Seeing Ben had arrived empty-handed, she quickly dropped it again. Ben gave her a consoling scratch behind the ears and received a sigh for his effort. "I fear my time away would not be as entertaining as you expect."

"Did you not venture away from the great burg of Newford?" Gavin asked.

"Aye."

"Then I'm certain your adventures will be entertaining enough."

There were murmurs of assent round the table and Cadan, who operated the local post office, crossed his arms. "Did you happen by the site of the new post office?" he asked. "I understand a fine parcel of land has been selected to replace the Lombard Street establishment. I'm curious to know if 'tis as promising as they say."

Ben took a swallow of his ale, but before he could reply, Jory interjected. "Tell me you didn't miss St. Paul's and the Whitechapel Bell Foundry."

"And I hope your entertainments took you past Threadneedle Street. The Bank, 'tis an impressive building in its own right."

This was from James. Owing to his banking interests, he was the only one of Ben's relations to make his own regular trips to London.

After several more similar statements, Ben lifted his hands in surrender. "Enough!" he said with a laugh as he wiped a bit of froth from his lip. It was always this way whenever he returned from one of his forays into London—his brothers and cousins peppering him with questions about this venue or that entertainment. "I did see many of these establishments," he assured them.

To Cadan, he replied, "The new site for the General Post Office *is* much improved over the Lombard Street location, if only by the mere fact that the mail coaches will have more room to turn about. I'm given to understand Mr. Smirke's design won't require them to queue in the street as they do at Lombard."

"And I happened to pass the Bank on Dividend Day. To be sure, James, I've never seen such a motley crowd as what came to collect their payments. But you aren't mistaken—Mr. Soane's building is pure and stately, with Corinthian columns larger than any in Truro."

He turned to Gryffyn, the stone carver among them. "You'd find much to admire in the entry, as 'tis topped with a magnificent and well-proportioned pediment."

"And, Jory, I'll never miss St. Paul's great cathedral or its bells, though I'm afraid I didn't have occasion to visit the Whitechapel foundry."

Jory crossed his arms, his coat stretching across his shoulders. "A pity," he said. "I'm told the tuning technique there is second to none."

"Before you ask," Ben said to Gavin, who served as parish constable, "I did *not* have occasion to visit Newgate."

Gavin snorted. "Given time, I feel certain you would have."

"But what about the entertainments?" Alfie asked as he frowned into his cider. "Didn't you take in the opera or the theater? Vauxhall, per'aps?"

Ben grinned. His oldest brother could be counted on to inquire into the more diverting aspects of his travels. "Of course," he replied. "You know one cannot go to London and miss the pleasure gardens. And Drury Lane has employed some ingenious techniques to improve the acoustics of the space."

"The acoustics?" Gavin asked with a frown.

Ben's relations were silent as they took this in. Alfie cast him a considering look that was a bit too astute for Ben's liking, so he amended, "And the actresses were comely."

"Though, to be sure," Gavin said to Alfie, "with your recent nuptials, there's little need to be considering such things."

"Aye," Alfie said, sufficiently diverted. "'Tis a fact that when you marry the love of your heart, all others fade from notice. Per'aps you'll learn it yourselves one day."

His unmarried cousins groaned at this while Jory and Gryffyn hid their smiles behind their cups. With his recent marriage, Ben's brother had exchanged his bachelorhood for expertise in all things to do with love and wedlock, which he was only too happy to impart to the rest of them.

Merryn, who'd remained silent during Ben's recounting of his time in London, watched from his place across the table. He unfolded his arms only to take a raspberry tart from the plate Peggy slid onto the polished oak. He was one of very few who knew the true purpose of Ben's travels. But given his cousins' questions—questions which had been suspiciously intent on London's architecture—Ben wondered if Merryn hadn't betrayed his confidence. His doubt lasted only a moment before he quickly dismissed the thought. He and Merryn might not agree on some things—or rather, most things—but his cousin wouldn't betray him.

It wasn't that Ben wished to dissemble with his relations, but the truth was more complicated than it ought to be. So instead, he allowed them to continue believing the fiction that he traveled to London on a lark, passing his time there with idle amusements until boredom and a lack of funds sent him home again. *That* was something they could easily credit.

When their questions finally wound down,

Merryn drained his ale and leaned forward, setting his cup on the table with a thump. "'Tis good to hear you've some knowledge of a working theater," he said. "My firm has been engaged by the Ladies' Society to design the sets for their new production. 'Tis to be something from Shakespeare, I believe."

"*Much Ado About Nothing*," Gavin said. "Or so I'm told. I hear I'm to play a role."

"As am I," Ben added with a frown.

"Excellent," Merryn said, and Ben grew wary. "I'm of a mind to give you the task of designing and building the sets. 'Twill be to your advantage if you're familiar with the tale."

Ben coughed. "You want me to design the sets?"

"I've taken on a number of new commissions near Truro," Merryn said. "'Twould be a considerable help to know I can leave this in your hands."

A theater production. Ben's mind immediately called up all that he'd seen in London, from the improved acoustics at Drury Lane to the gas lighting at Sadler's Wells. It leaped at the possibilities of such a project until the inherent problems made themselves known. He excelled at finding problems, and this endeavor had the potential for many.

Multiple sets would be needed in short order, to say nothing of the means to change them out quickly. There would be supplies to procure. A schedule to follow. And the ladies were sure to have a *budget*.

"Say you'll consider it," Merryn pressed.

His answer was an immediate *No*, but his relations looked on, waiting. He lifted his mug and spoke around one of his cavalier grins. "I shall think on it."

———

BRONWYN LOWERED HERSELF into the chair across from Wynne and waited while her cousin tallied a lengthy column of figures. The Feather's small office was generally well-ordered, but today it gave evidence of Newford's recent flood of incomers. A stack of leather-bound ledgers sat askew atop the desk, and a bin of tradesmen's bills was near to overflowing.

Bronwyn tidied the ledgers, squaring them on the desk as she knew Wynne preferred. The scratch of her cousin's pen paused on the page as Wynne eyed her movements. Bronwyn gave the ledgers one final tap just to see her cousin's eyes narrow, then she leaned back in her chair to wait.

Finally, Wynne set her pen in the stand and settled her hands atop the gentle swelling of her belly. Impending motherhood agreed with her cousin, whose pale features wore a pleasing radiance beneath her auburn curls. They were softer, as if drawn in chalk, and Bronwyn thought she'd never been in better looks.

"The Feather has been bustling of late," Bronwyn observed.

"Aye, that it has, but I'll not complain over the increase in custom. If I'd have known there were so many despairing ladies in the whole of England that they must journey to Newford to find their husbands, I'd have written my own Inventory long since."

Bronwyn agreed with a snort. "I've no doubt of that. You've a right talent for organizing a situation to its proper conclusion."

"'Taint so much a talent as a habit, and a dreadful one to hear my husband tell it."

Bronwyn laughed. "Roddie has come out the better for your organizing ways, so he's no room for complaint."

"And so I've told him." While Wynne's condition may have softened her edges, Bronwyn was pleased to see her boldness remained. Wynne tilted her head to one side and added, "I assume there's a purpose to this discussion. A situation you wish to organize, per'aps?"

Bronwyn shifted uncomfortably. "Not organize so much as encourage. I'll admit to being at a loss, and I thought you might have some advice." At her cousin's lifted brow, she drew a breath and continued. "'Tis clear for anyone to see the love Jory and Anna share. And yet, they mightn't have found one another again if you hadn't arranged matters so nicely."

"Love is infuriating when it meanders. I merely gave theirs a gentle nudge to move things along."

Bronwyn couldn't help her scoff. "Gentle? You threatened Anna with gaol when she couldn't pay her bill, and then you had her working for a pittance."

"A pittance? Not so much as that," Wynne said with an arch smile. "But I assume we're speaking now of your friend Kate?"

Bronwyn nodded.

"And…?"

"Well, Ben, of course. Although I've no wish to see either of them confined in gaol," she was quick to add.

"Aye. 'Tis a mystery how such a proper match is clear to everyone but the pair themselves."

Bronwyn shook her head. "To complicate matters, Kate's lately set her cap for—" She paused. She could hardly betray her friend's confidence, although she suspected this entire conversation might have been skirting the edges of that principle. "A particular gentleman," she finished.

"'Tis certainly an added difficulty," Wynne said.

"I suspect she can't see beyond the rosy haze of her ardor for this gentleman she's chosen?"

"The rosy haze of her *specifications* would be more fitting," Bronwyn corrected with an impatient wave of her hand. "I doubt very much 'tis ardor that's clouded Kate's vision."

"And this other gentleman, he's agreeable to a match?"

"He's not *dis*agreeable, but 'tis hardly the same thing."

Wynne tapped her chin with one finger. "And you're certain Kate doesn't hold her chosen gentleman in affection? I wouldn't wish to be meddlesome." At the not-so-subtle lift of Bronwyn's brows, she amended, "Overly meddlesome, rather."

"I don't believe she holds the gentleman in any true affection. She squares her shoulders like this"— Bronwyn demonstrated—"whenever she engages him in conversation, as if she must fortify her spirit for the task. 'Tis some painful to watch."

Bronwyn had often wondered if her brash interference at Copper Cove all those years before might have altered the natural flow of things for Kate and Ben. Back then, she'd thought only of reclaiming time with her new friend. Time which her cousin had seemed intent on commandeering for himself. She recognized the impulse now for envy, and she felt ashamed.

That she considered interfering again—had sought Wynne's counsel to that end, in fact—gave her pause, but something must be done. Though the notion of having Kate for a sister wasn't without its appeal, she couldn't bear to see her friend—or her brother, for that matter—marry for anything less than love.

Wynne pressed her lips in thought. "And Ben is equally unmovable, for reasons only he knows."

"I imagine our cousin is easy enough to sort," Bronwyn said. "Firstly, he's always treated Kate like a... well, like a princess. I think he's rather in awe of her."

"Hmm. A flaw of the worst sort, to be sure," Wynne said dryly.

"I freely admit I wouldn't mind having a pedestal of my very own," Bronwyn said. "I imagine it might grow tedious, but I'd like to confirm the fact for myself."

Wynne tipped her head at this logic. "And secondly?"

"Well, beyond the pedestal obstacle, have you ever known our cousin to follow anything through to its proper end? Ben is singularly accomplished at... avoiding accomplishment. 'Tis as if he fears..."

"Failing," Wynne said.

"Succeeding," Bronwyn finished at the same time.

"Aye." Wynne gave a considering rub to her

temple before she blew out a breath. "Those are some hedges to climb. 'Tis possible this is one field that can't be crossed."

Bronwyn's brow bent low. She'd not have expected Wynne to surrender so easily, softer edges notwithstanding. She was about to say as much when her cousin straightened, eyes lighting with inspiration.

"What they need is a common aim," Wynne said. "A shared task. Roddie and I grow closer as we manage the Feather. I suspect 'twould be the same for others."

With a groan, Bronwyn said, "Already considered. I hoped to see them cast together as Beatrice and Benedick, but Kate was having none of it. And now, *I'm* to play Beatrice."

Wynne snorted a soft laugh. *"You're* to play our cousin's *amour*? Don't Beatrice and Benedick share a kiss?"

"Aye. 'Tis meant to occur in the final scene, but Mrs. P has already pulled me aside with some strong direction. There's to be No Kissing. Which I suppose is to the good if I'm playing Beatrice. Kissing Ben would be akin to kissing Merryn." She rubbed a hand over her mouth as if that were enough to erase the thought, and a delicate, sympathetic shiver shook her cousin's shoulders.

"There may be other ways to bring our pair

together," Wynne mused. "I overheard your brother say he wishes Ben to design the sets. I imagine there will be romantic gardens and the like. To be sure, 'twill require a lady's perspective to see it done properly."

"Per'aps… but I don't see Ben agreeing to such a project, much less Kate volunteering to offer her counsel. She'd rather muck about with her flowers."

"And that," Wynne said, "is where you must learn the fine art of organizing."

CHAPTER SEVEN

A T THE START of the new week, Kate donned her best Sunday dress, a soft muslin stripe in the palest pink. The sleeves were short and puffed, the rounded neckline modest and trimmed with a dainty ruffle. The fabric draped to create a pleasing silhouette, and she wondered if Merryn would notice. He was unfailingly polite and generous with his compliments. Perhaps today was the day his admiration might cause her stomach to dip.

She turned her attention to the view outside her window as Mary finished putting up her hair. Ben's castle squatted atop its ridge, perfectly centered in the frame of her dark green curtains. Ivy-covered and nestled in a dense patch of wild roses, the sight of the small structure never failed to send an easy, calming warmth through her.

Mary finished with the pins, and Kate eyed her reflection in the mirror. She might not have a widow's sophistication, but Mary had done wonders with her hair. It would do. Lifting the lid on her glove box, she frowned at the interior.

"Mary, have you seen my Sunday gloves?"

"No, Miss Parker. Not since you wore 'em last week."

Kate frowned, a suspicion already forming. "Where is Alys?"

"Your sister has already left for the church with Miss Bronwyn."

With a silent press of her lips, Kate retrieved her second-best pair then went in search of her father. She found him in his rooms making notes in his journal while Henderson attempted to tie his cravat. "Mr. Parker, if you'll just hold your chin up a bit longer…"

Her father grumbled something unintelligible but obediently lifted his chin. He dropped it half a second later to make another notation in his book. Henderson let go the ends of the cravat with a frown.

"Perhaps I can finish," Kate said.

"You're welcome to try, Miss Parker." Henderson stepped aside to collect the shaving things and Kate approached her father.

"Papa, we must go soon."

"What's that?" His eyes remained on his book, and Kate prodded his chin with her finger until he looked up.

"The church, Papa. You know our vicar dislikes latecomers."

Her father gave his throat a gruff clearing. "Katie, the way he pontificates, he's fortunate to have any comers at all, late or otherwise."

"He's a vicar," she said reasonably as she smoothed the linen cravat against his collar. "I believe pontificating is part of the job. Now, tell me about your latest experiment with your new orchid while I finish your cravat. I believe you were testing different soils and exposures to encourage the bloom."

"Yes," he said, his journal forgotten for the moment. "Turns out, I was right about the ratio of chicken droppings." He lifted his chin and explained the results of his latest research as she wound and looped the ends of the cloth into a simple knot. He was still pontificating—their vicar would have been impressed—on the benefits of an eastern exposure versus western when she bundled him into his coat.

The day promised to be a fine one as the sun burned off the morning's mist and released the earthy scents of red campion, bluebells and wild leek. Birds flew from the hedgerows as the Parker carriage bowled along the narrow lane into

Newford. They soon reached the parish church holding up one end of the high street. Kate and her father descended near the lychgate to find much of the town already gathered in their dark suits and Sunday gowns. The air hummed with conversation and low laughter.

Her father soon sought the company of Dr. Rowe, a fellow plant enthusiast, and Kate's eyes instantly found a knot of Kimbrells, including Merryn's tall form. He stood with several of his relations near the churchyard's low stone wall, hands clasped behind his back.

His shoulders were broad and stretched to fill his coat while a strong jawline above the simple knot of his neckcloth hinted at a quiet confidence. In truth, she found him a trifle overwhelming, but she supposed that was to be expected of anyone a lady considered making a life with. One of his cousins said something to cause them all to laugh, and he smiled, revealing a tiny dent on one side of his mouth. It was a relief to know the man wasn't *too* serious.

How she wished to know his thoughts on matrimony. On matrimony as it related to *her*, specifically. She would like to know her chances of making a match sooner than later. For the merest moment, she imagined broaching the matter with him directly.

May I hear your sentiments regarding our

acquaintance? Do you foresee, by chance, an affection finding its way to your heart?

Her face quickly heated at the thought. It was too bold. No lady would be so forward. A widow might enjoy such freedoms, but certainly not an unmarried miss. A pair of sparrows scolded her noisily from the tree above.

She adjusted her bonnet, tucking a stray curl back into place before smoothing her skirts. Merryn's head came up and, catching her eye, he nodded politely. She returned his greeting with an equally courteous dip of her head. It was all very well done. Then, to her surprise, he broke from his companions and moved in her direction. Before she could prepare herself, he stood before her.

"Miss Parker." His eyes were a warm, kind green she'd always thought suited him. But then she considered her own dark brown ones and wondered—fleetingly—if their children might not have eyes the color of a stagnant pond.

"Mr. Kimbrell," she said a bit too quickly.

"'Tis a fine Sunday."

"One of the finest this spring, I believe. My father and his plants are especially pleased with the temperate weather we've enjoyed."

"What d'you suppose our vicar will address today with his sermon? To be sure, he's been going on about the divine state of matrimony lately."

Kate's breath hitched. "He—he has. I wonder if the theme is on account of Miss Darling's Inventory." Something cleverer seemed warranted, but before she could determine what that might be, Mrs. Matthews materialized before them. The widow wore a fetching straw bonnet and pale lavender gown. It was a shade that should have been ghastly on a woman of her coloring, but it only made the lady appear elegantly radiant. To further the point, Mrs. Matthews appeared quite graceful and no worse for her injured ankle.

"Mr. Kimbrell. Miss Parker," she said with a charming smile for each of them. Pleasantries were exchanged and then, returning her gaze to Merryn, she said, "Mr. Kimbrell, might I beg a moment of your time? I'm considering renovations to my morning room in London, and I wondered if I might seek your capable opinion."

"Certainly," he said, "though perhaps Miss Parker might join us to offer another lady's perspective."

He truly was the kindest of gentlemen to include her, but Kate had no wish to join a pitched battle for his attentions. "Thank you," she replied, "but I see your sister waving to me just over there." She ignored the way her shoulders eased to know their conversation was to be cut short.

Merryn left her with a courteous and—dare she

say apologetic—nod and that was that. Kate reflected on the facile way in which Mrs. Matthews had extracted him to her own purposes. It was a technique she should remember, if only she could bring herself to be so bold to beg a gentleman's time.

She hadn't misspoken regarding Bronwyn, who waved from across the churchyard as if she were signaling a ship. Her friend stood with Morwenna and Alys, and Kate was unsurprised to see her Sunday gloves gracing her sister's arms. This had been the way of it ever since Alys had left off her pinafores. Before she could begin making her way through the crowd, a low voice spoke from her side.

"What has you in such a taking?" It was Ben, and she recovered her smile to greet him.

"And a good morning to you," she said.

His lips tilted on one side, and his dark blue eyes brightened. "'Tis a good morning indeed. The sun warms the air, and not a cloud marks the sky. And yet, I can tell something displeases you."

"You're mistaken," Kate said, though her words lacked conviction. Whether by luck or sorcery, Ben had always been able to discern her moods, no matter how closely she guarded them.

"You'll not fool me," he said as he leaned close. "'Tis clear in the tilt of your eyes." His gaze dropped to her mouth as he added, "And your lips betray you."

"My—my lips?"

"Aye, you've the merest crease that forms just here." He lifted a hand to indicate the corner of her mouth but dropped it too soon. That was to say, he dropped it before he touched her.

Kate moistened her lips, which had gone dry.

Ben lifted his head to study the milling crowd. His gaze lingered on Merryn and Mrs. Matthews before moving to Alys. Eyes narrowing, he said, "Ah. The mouse has pinched your gloves again."

"How do you manage that?" Kate asked, her telltale lips forgotten.

Ben merely tapped the side of his head. "I've a keen eye and scads of siblings, so I know the trials you suffer. Shall I vanquish your foe, my lady?"

"What? Alys?"

"I can hold her while you strip the gloves from her arms."

His words and the image they produced startled a laugh from Kate, and she marveled at how easily he turned her irritation to amusement. "I thank you for your brave offer," she said, "but I don't think such measures will be necessary." She leaned toward him to confide, "Sisters have other means of retribution."

He gave a mock shiver. "'Tis fortunate then that I'm cursed only with brothers."

She smiled as the church bell rang a solemn, low-toned peal. The vicar and his curate pushed open the heavy wooden doors, and the assembled crowd shifted. Kate's eyes sought Merryn once more. He still stood with Mrs. Matthews. As she watched, he offered an arm and the lady took it.

"Kate?"

Ben's voice recalled her, and she turned to see he held his arm for her, waiting. With another smile for him, she settled her hand on his sleeve and allowed him to lead her inside.

———

BEN MATCHED HIS stride to Kate's shorter one as they entered the church, their footfalls echoing against the grey slate floor. The shadowed interior was a dark contrast to the sunny churchyard, and the combined scents of damp stone, tallow and wood polish filled the air.

Kate's hand was a soft, warm weight on his sleeve. She'd been careful to hide her thoughts on seeing Merryn with Mrs. Matthews. He didn't think anyone else had noticed the slight pinch between her brows, but her dismay only confirmed his suspicion: she'd developed an affection for his cousin. How or when it had happened, he couldn't say, but there was no denying the inevitability of it. Merryn was precisely the sort of gentleman Kate deserved. Respectable and accomplished. Steadfast. Ben had been accused of many things, but never that.

He led her to her family's bench and saw her seated before seeking his own place. The Kimbrells occupied seven rows near the pulpit. Their prominent position at the front of the church owed much to their family's influence in Newford. Ben suspected, however, that their vicar preferred the arrangement for other reasons, as it allowed him to keep a watchful eye on the less attentive members of his flock.

He found an empty place behind Alfie, who sat with his new bride. Alfie's hand held Eliza's, and his shoulder rubbed hers, though there was plenty of space on the bench beside them. Eliza leaned close to whisper something in Alfie's ear. The intimacy of the gesture and the easy contentment that sat his brother's shoulders sent a stab of envy through Ben, and he pulled his gaze from the pair. As he turned his hat in his hands, Merryn slid onto the seat beside him. Ben glanced at his cousin then shifted to give him room.

"Have you given any more thought to the theater sets?" Merryn asked rather predictably.

"I have," Ben said. And he'd sooner poke sticks in his eyes than take on such a task. There was no need to go borrowing trouble. But Merryn waited, brows lifted, so he said, "I don't think—that is, I've a number of matters requiring my time." Merryn's brows reversed course at this nonsense, so Ben finished with, "I'll have my answer for you d'rectly."

"There's little time to waste," Merryn said, also predictably. His cousin, unlike most of his relations, lived by his timepiece. "The work must begin this week."

"Aye," Ben replied automatically as he watched Mrs. Matthews take a seat with her companion. The benches, in fact, were full with ladies newly come to assess Newford's bachelor offerings.

Merryn leaned back and followed his gaze. "Alfie has set a fine example for us, marrying Miss Darling. D'you consider a similar fate?"

Ben gave his cousin a sardonic glance and crossed his arms. "I've no such plans." Then, swallowing against the dryness in his throat, he said, "D'you? Have you developed an affection for a particular lady, per'aps?"

Merryn's gaze left Mrs. Matthews to pass over the assembled parishioners. It lingered overlong on Kate's bench until he turned back to Ben. "An affection? No, but there are other reasons to marry."

Ben's brows stretched toward his hairline. "I assume you don't refer to ensuring our noble succession," he said dryly. "Pray, enlighten me."

"Why, I imagine a wife would make a home more comfortable."

"As would a housekeeper."

"And if I'm to compete with the more established firms in Truro, I'll need an engaging hostess. 'Twould require a bit more than a housekeeper's talents."

There was no disputing that Kate would make an admirable hostess, but Ben said only, "Depends on the housekeeper."

Merryn snorted in amusement. Belatedly, Ben recalled his cousins, in their boyhood daftness, had used the term "housekeeper" to refer to ladies of ill repute. They'd thought themselves clever and daring to speak of housekeepers within earshot of Newford's matrons. It wasn't until Mrs. Pentreath—who'd been old even then—pulled one of his cousins by the ear that they understood the term was a well-worn euphemism and their cleverness not so original as they'd thought.

Merryn's gaze returned to Mrs. Matthews once more, and Ben released his breath. His cousin had no more interest in Kate than he did any lady who might fill the role of hostess. He probably didn't even know that—despite the perfection of the roses in her garden—her favorite flowers were bluebells. She loved their wildness and pluck. Or that she had a tiny freckle just below the corner of her lip—had his cousin even noticed?

Ben gave his throat a clearing. Straightened and

unfolded his arms before turning his hat twice on his knee. Finally, he nodded in the direction of Mrs. Matthews. "Our latest visitor seems interested in pursuing your acquaintance."

"Hmm..." There was no inflection to indicate Merryn's thoughts on the matter.

"You should invite her to walk with you after the service."

The vicar rapped twice on the pulpit to signal the start of his sermon. "Per'aps," Merryn murmured as quiet fell over the church. Ben closed his eyes, certain Kate wouldn't appreciate his efforts, but what was he to do? Never had there been a more *un*suitable match than Merryn and Kate.

———

KATE ADJUSTED THE ribbons of her bonnet as she left the church with her family. The congregation mingled beneath the shade of the churchyard's great spreading beech while a pair of red-billed choughs called noisily from a lofty branch. Kate watched Merryn across the churchyard, his head tipped toward Mrs. Matthews *again*, when an arm looped swiftly through hers.

"You were late this morning," Bronwyn said.

"I couldn't find my gloves," Kate replied, narrowing her eyes at Alys. Her sister had the grace to blush, which was something at least. Alys was soon hailed by a group of her friends, and Kate and Bronwyn settled into a slow pace.

"The widow seems taken with her savior," Bronwyn said softly, a sympathetic twist to her expression.

Her words drew Kate's eye back to the pair. "Does he—do you think he returns her regard?"

"I don't know, but I imagine he'll not have the time to keep company with anyone soon." Kate drew back in inquiry and Bronwyn continued. "The Ladies' Society has engaged his firm to build the sets for our play. Mrs. P is even now seeking a volunteer from the ladies to coordinate the effort." Bronwyn nodded toward the lychgate, where Mrs. Pentreath was in earnest discussion with several matrons.

"Oh?" A long moment passed while her friend's words hung between them.

"Mrs. P seeks a volunteer," Bronwyn repeated, more slowly this time and with emphasis on each word.

Kate's mind, once it latched onto the possibilities, spun.

She'd made little progress in her campaign to gain Merryn's affections, but might this be the opportunity she needed? It was true, she had no wish to take a performer's role in the Ladies' Society production. That sort of activity was better suited to

Bronwyn, who adored dramatics, but Kate *had* studied the play years before with her governess. She could advise Merryn on the sets that would be needed. They might develop an easier accord in one another's company.

Perhaps then, she might finally know the direction of his thoughts where she was concerned. At the very least, she'd gain an advantage over Mrs. Matthews. She resisted the urge to rub her temple. Why must matrimony be such an endeavor?

At the lychgate, Mrs. Pentreath left her companions, a frown marring her brow. She'd not had any success persuading one of them to her purpose, it would seem.

Kate's eyes found Merryn once more, and she was dismayed to see him walking toward the Feather. He'd extended an arm, and Mrs. Matthews' hand rested on his sleeve as she and her companion walked with him along the high street.

"Kate?" Bronwyn said.

Kate cleared her frown. "I must speak with Mrs. Pentreath." Her stomach dipped uncomfortably as she turned and strode across the churchyard.

———

BEN LEFT THE church's cool interior and replaced his hat. He was pleased to see Merryn walking ahead with Mrs. Matthews, although his conscience pinched at him for his part in his cousin's new interest.

Several of his brothers waited near his father's wagon to make the journey up the hill to his grandfather's home. Sunday afternoons were for food and family.

Bronwyn fell into step beside him. "Are you away to Oak Hill?" she asked.

"Aye. You?"

She nodded. "Have you been practicing your lines for the play?"

Ben sighed. It was unlikely he'd escape his fate as the Bard's Benedick. "No."

She frowned in annoyance before allowing, "There's still time yet. Oh, did you hear Morwenna's agreed to manage the costumes? And I understand the Ladies' Society has engaged Merryn's firm to build the sets."

His cousin's tone had gone swiftly from annoyed to friendly, and he was instantly suspicious.

"I'm aware," he said slowly.

"I believe Kate, in fact, has just volunteered to coordinate the effort." Bronwyn crossed her arms. It was a stance she took when she was being disingenuous, and he narrowed his eyes.

"She has?"

A nod and then, "I imagine 'twill take some time to see the sets done properly."

Ben rubbed the back of his neck, but he didn't respond.

Bronwyn, undeterred, continued. "Days, most likely. Weeks, even."

And with that, his imagination took hold of his thoughts, painting vivid pictures he'd no wish to consider. Kate, head bent as she and Merryn worked on the sets together. The pair of them, studying his cousin's drawings. Kate might brush Merryn's sleeve as she pointed out a change that was needed.

There was no question but that Merryn would find an admirable hostess in Kate, but at what expense to her? He didn't imagine his cousin was so unfeeling to marry a lady *solely* for her hostessing skills, but hadn't he just heard it from Merryn's own lips?

A weight settled in Ben's stomach. He had no desire to take on the sets, but how could he refuse if it meant protecting Kate's heart? He closed his eyes for the length of one long-drawn breath.

When he opened them again, a smile lurked at the corner of Bronwyn's lips. He was certain she must be up to something, but he didn't have the time or the desire to sort her machinations. He turned and left her, striding toward the high street.

"Where are you going?" she called behind him.

"I need to speak with Merryn. Tell my father I'll be along d'rectly."

CHAPTER EIGHT

THE NEXT DAY, Kate entered Newford's newly built theater, a modest timber structure wedged between Dr. Rowe's surgery and the smithy. Mrs. Pentreath had suggested Kate arrive early so work might begin on the sets "forthwith." A golden wedge of morning sunlight narrowed then disappeared as the doors closed behind her. The tangy scents of turpentine and sawdust hung on the air, and candlelit sconces lit the way to even rows of benches that stretched toward the low stage. Though lamps were also hung, Mrs. Pentreath had expressly prohibited their use as "whale oil is far too dear."

Squire Carew's youngest daughter, who had volunteered to play the beautiful Hero, stood in the center of the stage with constable Gavin Kimbrell. Kate smiled to see Ben wasn't the only Kimbrell gentleman who'd been conscripted for a role in the production.

Miss Carew's voice carried as she practiced the scene. Her eyes turned soft—there was no other word for it—as she delivered her lines with practiced sighs while her maid stitched quietly on one of the benches. Gavin, for his part, appeared decidedly uncomfortable with the lady's effort. Kate could only assume he'd been tasked with the role of Claudio, Hero's romantic love interest.

As the pair continued their recitation, Kate studied the stage's dimensions. She'd spent the previous evening re-reading the play's first act and making notes. She'd even drawn sketches of a few of the garden scenes. If she were to assist Merryn, she didn't wish to appear ill-prepared.

Her heart thumped nervously. Of course, she and Merryn had exchanged polite, everyday sorts of conversations over the years, but she'd never spent so much time in his company as she was about to do. What if he found her ideas simple or ridiculous? Or worse, what if she compared unfavorably to Mrs. Matthews' Town polish?

Though Kate could boast a marquess in her lineage, that had been two generations ago. And besides, the Kimbrells were a remarkably democratic lot, favoring good sense and character over such things as pedigrees. A marquess wouldn't sway a man like Merryn.

Kate sighed and pressed her notebook to her chest. Not for the first time, she wondered if she'd made a mistake in volunteering to assist with the sets. She'd never thought forming an attachment with an eligible gentleman would be so difficult or require so much... strategy, but the gentlemen of Newford were nothing if not slow to the pursuit. She felt like one of Wellington's officers, mustering the troops to greatest advantage.

Miss Carew finished her scene with the constable, and Gavin escorted her down the short steps. "How did we do?" Miss Carew asked as they drew near.

In truth, Kate thought Miss Carew's portrayal of the modest and gentle Hero had been a bit overdone, but she smiled and said, "I'm certain you'll make a fine Hero to our constable's Claudio."

"You're kind to say so," the lady said, her eyes shining beneath the praise. "But the constable has the role of Leonato. Mr. Cadan Kimbrell is to play Claudio."

Kate hid her surprise and turned to Gavin. "You're playing the part of Leonato? Hero's father?"

The constable lifted one brow and replied flatly, "Aye."

Miss Carew's declarations had definitely been a bit too breathy then. Certainly, Kate had never

spoken thusly to her own father, and judging by the
flush in the constable's cheeks, he was of a similar
mind. "I see," she said. "Well, your performance
was... captivating, Miss Carew."

The lady beamed her pleasure before extending
an invitation. "My father is to host a supper, and we
mean to invite all those involved in the play. He
says it's the tradition for all the best theaters in
London. The invitations will go round soon, but do
say you'll come, Miss Parker."

Kate thanked Miss Carew for the invitation and
assured her she would be pleased to attend. The
pair took their leave, Gavin excusing himself for
"constable business" and Miss Carew collecting her
maid.

"Your performance was captivating, Miss
Parker."

Kate jumped at the low voice behind her. "Ben!"
she scolded as she pressed a hand to her throat.
"You gave me a fright."

He brushed her words aside. "Why didn't you
say what you truly thought of Miss Carew's
performance?"

"Why didn't I—did you *hear* it? I don't think I
could have offered a criticism Miss Carew wouldn't
have found offensive."

"Of course, you could have. You always know
the proper thing to say."

Kate stared at him, certain he must have suffered a head injury on his way to the theater. "I *never* know the proper thing to say," she corrected him.

"Well, you do with me." His mouth hitched in one of his familiar, lopsided smiles.

"Yes, but speaking with you is an easy matter."

"I'm pleased to hear it. Now," he said, turning his attention to the stage. "How shall we begin?"

"What do you mean?"

"The sets. Where shall we start?"

Kate frowned in confusion. "Where's your cousin? I thought Merryn was engaged to design the sets."

It was Ben's turn to frown. "No one's told you then?"

"I—no. Told me what?"

He hesitated, and the light in his eyes dimmed a bit. "'Tis true, Merryn's *firm* has been engaged to design the sets, but in his questionable wisdom, my cousin has turned the task over to me."

———

KATE'S MOUTH FORMED a delicate O of surprise, and Ben cursed his stupidity. What had he been thinking to take on the sets for Merryn? That Kate wouldn't notice the change? That she would be pleased by it? Her dismay on learning Ben was to be her partner in this endeavor might have been humorous if it didn't cause a dull ache to settle behind his ribs. Was her heart truly so set on his cousin?

He swallowed. It wasn't too late to change his course. The work hadn't begun yet. Merryn could find another to build the sets, or he could take on the blasted task himself. Perhaps then he might find a genuine affection for Kate. To be sure, retreat would be the honorable course, and Ben was very accomplished at retreat.

But then Kate smiled, swiftly tucking her surprise behind the gentle curve of her lips. She gave his forearm a squeeze, and he was hard-pressed to recall her disappointment when she said, "Oh, we'll have the best fun. I can't think of anyone I'd rather work with."

The ache in his chest eased the tiniest bit, and he forgot about retreat and honor. He might tell himself he was a hero, saving Kate from a loveless match with his cousin, but even he wasn't such an accomplished liar as that.

CHAPTER NINE

KATE COULDN'T HAVE been more surprised to learn Ben would design their sets than if he'd announced a sudden wish to sail to China. In all the years of their acquaintance, she'd rarely known him to take on such a task. Indeed, it was a well-known fact throughout Newford that Benedick Kimbrell did not begin such things, much less finish them.

But her surprise, though great, was eclipsed by an even more profound sense of... relief. Tension eased from her shoulders like morning mist dissolving beneath the sun's warmth. The tightness in her chest lessened, and she pulled in a full, restoring breath. She'd have to find another way to engage Merryn's interest now, but that was a worry for another day.

Never had there been a lady more lacking in

fortitude, but at the moment, she couldn't find it in herself to care.

The doors to the theater opened and several more people entered, chatting excitedly about their roles. "Let's have a seat and discuss our plans," Ben said, motioning to one of the benches.

"I took the liberty of preparing some drawings," she began as she settled her skirts about her. "I believe we can capture the charm of Leonato's villa quite easily." She turned the pages of her notebook, quickly passing the more elaborate sets she'd imagined until she found an uncomplicated arrangement. As disloyal as she felt thinking it, if they wished to see Ben's sets completed in time for the production, it would be best to keep things simple. She turned the notebook so he could see her sketch.

He leaned closer, his shoulder warm against hers as he studied the page. "You're thinking we should prepare a painted backdrop for the garden scenes."

"Yes, I thought we might bring some potted plants from my father's glasshouse as well. Perhaps we can paint a vibrant blue sky above and fit a bench or a fountain there on the far side."

"'Twould be simple enough," he agreed, thumb and forefinger stroking his chin. Then he took her book and thumbed backwards. He stopped at one of the pages she'd passed, and his brow bent in concentration. "What's this?" A muscle jumped in his jaw, and Kate was struck by the seriousness of his countenance. It was an expression she was unaccustomed to seeing on his face.

"It's nothing," she assured him as she reached for the book. "Merely some ideas I was considering."

"D'you like the notion of a balcony then?" He extended his arm, holding the book from her reach as he assessed the stage before them. "I imagine Beatrice could deliver some of her more cutting lines from above. 'Twould be more dramatic that way."

Kate considered him. She'd thought a fountain a bit of a stretch, but a balcony... Ben was intelligent, articulate and capable of many things. Building a balcony—a complete balcony, rather—was probably not one of those things. "I imagine a balcony would be... ambitious," she said gently.

After a long moment, he returned the book to her. "Aye."

This was accompanied by a shrug. The motion was the same careless hitch of one shoulder he'd offered many times before, but this time something shifted in his eyes. Something at odds with his devil-may-care demeanor. Something that resembled... disappointment. But that couldn't be right. Ben, who had few aims in life, was rarely disappointed.

Against her better sense, Kate said slowly, "A balcony *would* be lovely, though. Do... do you think it could be done?"

"A balcony would be a proper challenge in the best of circumstances, and 'twould cost a good stub. Mrs. Pentreath assures me there's a firm budget, and the Ladies' Society will not go a ha'penny more."

Kate nodded. Mrs. Pentreath had warned her of the same. "Yes. Of course, you're right. A simple backdrop will be much more sensible."

Ben removed his own notebook from his coat and turned to a fresh page. "I'll start a list of supplies," he said. "Should we meet again tomorrow?"

Kate nodded, but her attention wasn't on Ben's words. She was certain she'd caught the lines of beautiful arches and intricate columns as he'd turned the pages of his own notebook. In all the years she'd known him, he'd always loved to sketch—swift and sweeping renderings of a bird or a tree or a fine prospect overlooking the sea. He'd often carried his notebook about for that very purpose. But the glimpses she caught as his pages flashed by seemed detailed and precise and far more ambitious than she'd have credited her friend with.

———

"GO." BEN POINTED at the door as his twin brothers waged a minor skirmish in his room. They froze to hear such a serious tone coming from their elder brother, who was more likely to start minor skirmishes than end them.

They lay atop his bed in a proper tangle of adolescent limbs, Daniel's arms locked fast about Matthew's throat, both faces flushed from their efforts. At least one eye was already starting to blacken. Ben might have found the sight humorous—he might have joined their game at one time—but when one corner of the bed crashed to the floor beneath their struggles, he rose from his desk and pointed at the door more emphatically.

Grumbling, his brothers got to their feet. "I told him he'd regret missing his supper," Daniel muttered.

"No, 'tis a woman that has him all teasy, to be sure."

"D'you think so? Per'aps he should hire himself a housekeeper."

Ben ran both hands through his already disordered hair as his brothers left him. With eight males living in his father's house, it was often an impossible feat to hear one's thoughts. This didn't usually pose a problem, as it was a rare day when Ben wished to hear his own thoughts. Today, though, he wouldn't have minded hearing *something*. A muse's whisper wouldn't have been unwelcome.

Thunder rumbled from a spring storm and needles of cold rain struck the window. It was all rather dramatic and a perfect reflection of his low mood. He'd been staring at the same page for the better part of the afternoon and evening, and he was no closer to his goal than when he'd sat down to sketch. Oh, he'd drawn plenty of balustrades and pilasters, but he wasn't pleased with the scale or proportion. Or the cost or ease of building or a multitude of other things. This one was too English, that one not Italian enough. They were all wrong.

In search of inspiration, he retrieved his London sketchbooks from his trunk. He'd enjoyed a prolific few weeks before returning to Cornwall, but none of his latest drawings fired his imagination. Then he thought of Kate's heart-shaped face and dark eyes as she'd gazed up at him. *A balcony would be lovely.* With rare determination, he stoppered his doubts and lowered his pencil to the page once more.

A balcony, he thought with a sigh. My kingdom for a balcony.

———

THE NEXT MORNING dawned clear, the sky having been wiped clean by a crisp spring wind. Kate patted the damp ground beneath the rose cutting she'd just planted but straightened at the sound of the garden gate opening behind her. She turned, quickly tucking her bare hands behind her back.

It was Ben, carrying his notebook and a crooked smile. His cheeks were ruddy, his hair disheveled when he removed his hat. He'd always had a curl above his right brow that refused taming, and the day's wind was having its way. There was a sharp energy about him, as if he'd harnessed a bit of sunlight, and Kate's lips curved in greeting.

"Good morning," she said. "I thought we were supposed to meet at the theater." As she spoke, she brushed at her hands behind her skirts.

"I've come to offer my escort, if you're agreeable. We can collect Bronwyn on the way down." He opened his mouth to say something more then closed it again. "What have you got behind your back?" he asked with no little suspicion.

"My—my back?"

"Yes. You're standing with your hands behind your back, looking as guilty as one of my brothers."

Her brows lifted in her best imitation of her grandmother. "I assure you, my conscience is clear."

"Then let me see your hands."

A long beat passed while Kate stared at him, the corner of her lip tucked behind her teeth. A bird took up a song nearby, and Ben waited as if he had no better things to do with his time.

"I've nothing better to do," he said and she frowned at how easily he read her thoughts.

Then the ridiculousness of the situation caused a

laugh to bubble up in her chest. They were at a draw, over gloves, of all things. Or the lack of gloves, rather. Were he anyone else, she would have been mortified to be caught with soil staining her fingers. But then, were he anyone else, he wouldn't have made such an impolite charge.

Before she could confess, though, he drew near then feinted to one side, reaching for her hands. She leaped back with a squeak, hands pressed tight behind her. The garden wall was at her back, six feet of warm male before her. He grinned in silent challenge, and she slowly pulled her hands to the front to reveal her dirt-stained fingers.

"Egads," he said in exaggerated horror. He lifted one of her hands, his palm warm against her bare skin. "Why don't you wear the gloves I brought you? Are they too large after all?"

She was caught. How to explain that, no matter how lovely the gloves, there was nothing to compare to the feel of rich soil or velvet-soft petals beneath one's fingers?

"They fit perfectly," she assured him. "Only, they're too fine to sully."

"Kate." He said her name with the certainty of one aware he'd been handed a falsehood.

"And," she conceded slowly, "I prefer to feel the earth."

His bafflement was immediate. "Whatever for?"

"It's silly, truly, but I can better tell what the flowers need this way. With cotton or leather between my hands and the soil, I may as well be blindfolded." She folded her hands before her, concealing the dirt beneath her nails as his thoughts played across his face. "I know it's poorly done—" she added, but he interrupted with a wave of his hand.

"No, no. 'Tis only that I must adjust my perception of the world, now that I know Miss Catherine Parker does not, in fact, defy the dirt."

She snorted—there was no other word for it. Her grandmother's scowl would have been fierce to hear such an unrefined sound from her. "You're horrid to tease me."

———

KATE WASHED THEN she and Ben collected Bronwyn. Their conversation on the lane down to Newford was easy, as it ought to be between friends. Once they arrived at the theater, Bronwyn left them to discuss costumes with Morwenna, and Ben turned to Kate. "The sets," he said, lifting his notebook. "You've two choices."

Her answering grin was swift at the reminder of the game he'd often played in their youth. He would offer two choices: peppermint or licorice? A crown of daisies or a wreath of heather? And then he'd proceed to grant her choice, dropping a peppermint into her waiting hand or weaving a crown of heather to place atop her head. It had always seemed a lark to him, to deliver her heart's desire with a flourish as if he were a loyal subject to her Queen Bess. And she'd been amused by his offerings, though they'd been but minor things.

Until his castle, rather.

The year she turned sixteen, she'd caught a chill in the damp of spring. She'd been dismayed to find herself confined to the front parlor while the wildflowers burst to life all around them. Ben had faithfully entertained her with amusing stories until one afternoon, he'd leaned toward her with a bracing grin. "We can't have your spirits brought low, so I offer you two choices."

Then, as now, she hadn't been able to stop her smile. "Tell me," she'd urged.

"A grand sailing ship or a regal castle?"

"Why, a castle, of course," she said with a weak laugh. "What would a lady do with a sailing ship?"

He gave her a resolute nod and left her to her tea. She'd been uncertain how he meant to grant such a lofty wish. She thought perhaps he would sketch a castle for her, but the next day, she watched him drive his father's cart laden with stones to the flat ridge opposite her window.

He spied her watching and saluted across the distance. She laughed at his teasing but quickly sobered as a structure slowly emerged from the thick gorse. Over the next months, it evolved bit by bit into a magnificent shape—squat on one end with a charming tower on the other. And all crafted of creamy golden stone that shone when the sun found it. It was such a grand and impulsive gift, and so like Ben.

"You ought to be an architect," she told him one afternoon. Ben had been enjoying their cook's seed cake as Kate idly thumbed the sketches in his notebook. But at her words, he'd merely shrugged and turned the subject, carefully taking his drawings back from her.

He'd never finished his castle. She was no expert, but it hadn't seemed there was much left to be done. A bit more roof atop the tower. A few more stones to finish the battlement, perhaps. But he'd left it all the same, as he did most things. His energy was high—infectious, even—until something else caught his fancy. And so it had been with his castle.

"Merryn needs my assistance with Dr. Rowe's new surgery," he'd said when she asked after his progress. "'Twill be some weeks before I can return to the folly."

Kate had grown used to the unfinished silhouette with its imperfect edges. And, as nature began to reclaim the space, she found even more to love about its ivy-covered battlements and the wild roses that bloomed with abandon along its walls. It was quite the loveliest sight to open her eyes to each morning.

Now, she and Ben found their seats on one of the theater's benches, and the same anticipation for the game filled her. "Tell me," she said. She bit her lip in curious anticipation as he turned the pages of his notebook.

"For the garden scenes, we can prepare a simple garden backdrop as we discussed or... we can build a working balcony."

He found the page he wanted and turned it for her. Kate's eyes widened. He'd drawn inspiration from her vague and inexpert drawings and added his own details. His sketch was precisely done with perfect scale and perspective. It depicted the courtyard of an Italian villa with lush gardens below and an ornate stone balcony above. Rich architectural details lent an air of authenticity to the image. He'd included vines crawling along the balcony rail and doors leading to the villa's interior. There were flowers and lamps for lighting and a *tree* to give the impression of height. She didn't recognize it as the stage that lay before them, so effectively had he rendered another world entirely.

She was silent for a long moment, dimly aware

of Ben sitting motionless beside her. His head was down, his gaze fixed on the page before them, but she sensed his tension. "It's… it's magnificent," she finally whispered as she traced the edge of the balcony with her finger.

She looked up in time to catch him sliding a glance toward her from the corner of his eye. "'Tis probably too much."

She nodded slowly. "It's ambitious, to be sure, but if it could be done, it would be breathtaking. It would capture our audience's imagination until they forget they're in Newford." She licked her lips and swallowed. "*Can* it be done?" she whispered, thinking of the unfinished castle beyond her bedroom window.

"Aye." His smile tipped up in a crooked grin.

His enthusiasm was catching, but Kate held herself in check. They weren't discussing a castle for Kate's amusement but a theater set which all of Newford required if the play was to be a success. So, she clarified, "Can it be done in time for the play?"

He hesitated briefly before nodding.

"And within the Ladies' Society budget?" she pressed.

He frowned. Ben had never been one for rules, but he nodded grudgingly.

If he were right… if it could be done… why, it would be spectacular. Surely, Truro's productions didn't boast anything half so lovely. Still, this was Ben. Ben, who'd always held a piece of her heart, but whose only ambition had ever been to amuse and entertain. She'd no wish to see him fail at the task. The thought of it caused her heart to trip, so she said cautiously, "And the remaining scenes... there will still be time enough—and funds—to complete the sets for them as well?"

"Aye," he said, leaning forward. "The remaining scenes can be set with painted backdrops and the exchange of a few props, but the balcony..." He stood and paced the length of the stage, using his hands to draw a structure only he could see. "I'll design it on a revolving platform to create two sets in one. The villa's ballroom will be on one side and the garden on t'other. 'Twill be a fitting place for the lovers' most romantic scenes."

Kate's cheeks heated at his words, but she couldn't deny the allure of what he proposed. When he stopped before her, she knew a sudden urge to embrace him, but she held her arms to her waist.

"Two choices," he reminded her.

"Why, the balcony, of course," she said readily.

CHAPTER TEN

ONCE KATE AND Ben were decided on the balcony, he immediately set to work taking measurements and jotting figures in his notebook. Kate was intrigued by the rather studious expression that gathered on his face as he scratched his pencil across the paper.

She wouldn't have believed it of her friend if she hadn't seen it for herself. At times, his intensity seemed a bit fevered, and more than once she'd caught him frowning at some figure or another on the page before him.

While he worked, she assisted Bronwyn to prepare lists of costumes and other items that would be needed. By the time Ben offered to escort them to their homes, the sun had fallen low in the sky to paint a golden wash over the landscape above Newford.

They rounded the final curve above Kate's home, and her steps slowed when she saw their groom unhitching a team from a traveling coach. The vehicle's black lacquered finish was dulled with dust, the wheels caked with mud from a long journey. A gold crest painted on the side left observers in no doubt of its passenger. Her grandmother had arrived.

Kate made a rapid, silent review of her person. There was plenty with which to find fault. Though her gown and bonnet were unexceptional for the walk to and from Newford, they were not in the first stare of fashion. And her fingers, though free of the morning's dirt, were ink-stained from the lists she and Bronwyn had written out.

She had some repairs to make before she could greet her grandmother, but at least she'd had the foresight to organize a proper supper. For the past week, the staff had been on alert, ready with menus and a full larder for Lady Catherine's imminent arrival.

"Your grandmother's arrived?" Bronwyn said as their steps came to a full stop.

Kate found her smile. "It would seem so." Inspiration struck, and she turned to her companions. "Why don't you both join us for supper?" There was safety in numbers, and the thought of entertaining her grandmother with friends at her side was immeasurably more appealing than the alternative. Though she would be sure to suffer some degree of mortification, it would be nothing to the uncomfortable interrogation she'd receive without the buffering protection of Company.

"I'm sorry," Bronwyn said with a wince. "I'm afraid I've a prior engagement."

Kate frowned at this cowardice.

"I do," Bronwyn insisted. "I'm to help Morwenna organize her ribbons. They become incredibly tangled, you know, what with all the people inspecting them for purchase."

Kate turned to Ben, lifting a brow in expectation. "And you? Do you also have a prior engagement? Neckcloths to sort, perhaps?"

Ben opened and closed his mouth before saying, "I don't think your grandmother approves of me."

"Of course, she does," Kate said, although the wry twist of Ben's lips indicated he saw through the lie. She didn't explain that her grandmother would find fault with *any* of the gentlemen in Newford because that seemed, well, insulting. But the Lady Catherine Dunne had grown from roots firmly planted and watered in the midland county of Leicestershire. Cornwall, by comparison, was so far removed from the rest of England "it may as well be on the moon." That Lady Catherine even deigned to visit her daughter's children was a tremendous honor indeed.

Ben's jaw tightened, and she could see him weighing her censure against that of her grandmother, a lady whose formidability was well known, even on the moon. It was clear who would win the battle for Ben's allegiance.

With a sigh, she straightened her spine and prepared for the evening ahead, but Ben surprised her.

"What time d'you dine?"

Kate's spirits lifted. "Seven sharp."

———

THAT EVENING, BEN approached the Parkers' polished oak door and wondered what madness had prompted him to agree to dine with Dragon Dunne. Although, in truth, Kate's grandmother was more properly addressed as Lady Catherine Dunne. Daughter of the Marquess of Wentworth and a Formidable Lady in her own right. He recalled her as a sharp-nosed woman with a tendency to speak in Capitals.

But Kate had invited him, and he couldn't have left her to suffer alone when it was within his power to—Well. He didn't know what power he wielded, but surely, he could be of some comfort to her during this trying time.

The Parkers' manservant opened the door on noiseless hinges before taking Ben's coat and hat. The house, which normally hummed with a relaxed energy, was silent as a tomb. Not even a maid could be seen, and Ben suspected they'd all been conscripted to the kitchen.

"Has someone died, Henderson?" he asked in an attempt at levity, though he was only half joking.

"Not yet, sir." The man didn't betray his humor by so much as the tick of an eyelash, and Ben held any further comment.

Henderson led him across the marble to the front parlor. Ben had been a frequent guest of the Parkers over the years and was unused to being presented so formally, but all the rules changed when Dragon—Lady Catherine, rather—came to visit. Henderson paused before the entry, casting a glance at Ben as if to assure himself the lamb was ready for the slaughter, before pulling the doors open with a soft swish.

Henderson announced him to the room, and Ben entered to find Kate's father standing at the window, a nearly empty glass in one hand. Kate and Alys rose from their chairs while a distinguished matron of advanced years remained seated on the striped settee. Lady Catherine's silver hair was immaculately coiffed, her silk gown finely cut, and the thick scent of lavender hung in the air. A white mop of a dog with a jeweled collar sat on the throne of Lady Catherine's lap.

The pair surveyed him with an imperious chin-tilt (the lady's) and a half-lidded gaze of disdain (the mop's, although it, too, could have been attributed to the lady). The tableau had all the appearance of a queen receiving her vassals. That Kate had sprung from such origins and didn't carry a bit of superiority about her was a feat that would forever amaze him.

Her father crossed the carpet to greet him, and Ben shook the man's hand before turning to the ladies. "Kate"—he stopped and corrected himself—"Miss Parker, thank you for the invitation to dine. And Miss Alys, how d'you fare this evening?"

Alys dipped into a perfect curtsy and replied, "Very well, Mr. Kimbrell, thank you." She gave every appearance of a demure miss ready for her first season, if not for the impertinent sparkle in her eye.

"Grandmother," Kate said. "You may recall Mr. Benedick Kimbrell from your previous visits to Cornwall."

"I'm old, Catherine, not Senile."

The great irony of a society that prided itself on its manners was that its members would ignore them so cavalierly. Kate, though she lacked the title, was tenfold the lady her grandmother was.

Nevertheless, he gave Lady Catherine a respectful bow, and the dog lifted its head to bare tiny, sharp teeth at him. He took a step back and said, "'Tis a pleasure to make your acquaintance once again, Lady Catherine."

Her eyes raked him. He couldn't be certain if she inspected the cut of his coat, his posture, or his very character. He thought perhaps she might have assessed all three in that single, efficient gaze.

Lady Catherine's tone held a touch of accusation as she said, "Your grandfather is Alan Kimbrell."

"Aye," he replied before he could offer a more refined *Yes*. He was that surprised she'd deemed the knowledge worthy enough to put away.

"Don't doubt that I've made my inquiries. Is he any less of a Scoundrel than he was thirty years ago? They've had Tales of him as far as Nottingham."

"I'll grant he's still a charmer, but I believe my grandmother, while she lived, had a smoothing effect on his rougher edges. He's found a measure of peace in his respectability."

"And which of the sons is your father?"

"Alfred Kimbrell, my lady."

Lady Catherine pursed her lips. "Ah, yes. You're The One who built that ridiculous folly."

"Grandmother!" Alys whispered as Kate offered him a pale expression of apology.

A fire burned in the hearth although there was

no need for it, and Ben clasped his hands behind his back so he wouldn't be tempted to tug at his collar. "Aye, one and the same," he confirmed with one of his most charming smiles. And then, because Kate looked so miserable, he added, "And you're very astute, my lady. 'Ridiculous' is an apt description, for it could never hope to match the architecture of the Midlands. Your county lays claim to some magnificent Jacobean specimens, I believe. The ruins of Grace Dieu Priory are an especially stunning example of the fine eye of your forefathers."

Lady Catherine eyed him as if *he* were the specimen before releasing him from her hook with a "Hrmph."

"Grandmother," Kate said as she retook her seat and smoothed her skirts. "Please tell us about your journey. I hope it was a pleasant one."

Ben claimed the empty chair next to Alys as Henderson—good chap—pressed a glass of port into his hand. Parker, he noted, had moved back into position near the window. He suspected the man were wishing himself back in his glasshouse. Ben wouldn't have minded joining him there.

"It was *not* a Pleasant Journey," Lady Catherine replied. "As you well know, traveling such great distances never agrees with me, but Needs Must. I'll do my duty to avoid an encore of the Tragic Events of 1814."

Ben thought back to the year in question. Surely, Lady Catherine couldn't mean—

Alys leaned toward him to whisper, "The Year of the Forgotten Season."

Ben recalled it well. The spring had been especially cold, and Kate shivered in her pelisse as they walked along the ridge near Kimbrell's Folly. She'd been in a brown study and, at his prompting, she finally confessed that her father had taken himself off for a month-long lecture series in York. Something about ferns or mosses, he thought. She'd learned of her parent's unexpected departure from their housekeeper, of all people.

"But weren't you to spend the season in Bath?" he'd asked. She responded with a delicate but alarming sniff, and Ben had felt a curious sting behind his own eyes as he hastily extended his handkerchief.

Kate had waved the offered linen aside with a smile and pretty excuses for her father's inattentiveness. She would be polite to the end—he imagined she'd even thank her hangman for assisting with the noose. He remembered thinking at the time that, despite her dirt-defying elegance, he and Kate weren't so different. The pair of them wielded their smiles as well as any shield.

"Your duty, Grandmother?" Kate asked now.

"I must ensure that Alys will be prepared to

make her bow when the time comes." Alys straightened until her grandmother added with a frown, "Though it seems there's still a good bit of Work To Be Done in that quarter."

Alys opened her mouth on this, and Ben held his breath until she wisely closed it again.

"There's little time to waste," Lady Catherine said repressively. "You must strike while you still have The Bloom Of Youth. We'll have no more delayed seasons." This last she directed toward the window, and Kate's father frowned into his glass, which was now empty. He mumbled something about moss and lichen and moved toward the decanter.

"As it stands," Lady Catherine continued, "your sister is left to make do with whatever match she can secure among the Local Populace. I can't like it, but there's nothing for it now." A glance at Ben and her gaze sharpened. "Your relation—the one who built the Methodists' new church near Truro— what's his name? Martin? Merlin?"

Ben cleared his throat. "'Tis Merryn Kimbrell, my lady."

She frowned. "An unusual moniker. Are you certain?"

"Quite."

"Hmm." The mop shifted in silent agreement, and Lady Catherine smoothed a bejeweled hand over his white fur. "He's in trade, so there's that against him, but I heard his name more than once in Bath. They say he's Prospects and a Future ahead of him. But you'll need to move quickly, Catherine. Time waits for no woman."

The flickering candlelight tossed shadows upon the rug. Kate's face was unreadable, though her cheeks were pink, and Ben wondered what she made of this. Would she confess to a growing affection between herself and Merryn?

Her father spoke from his position by the window. "There's still time for Katie to find an agreeable match, if that is her wish." The ladies seemed surprised by his presence and even more so by his defense.

Lady Catherine's snort cut the air like an arctic wind. "Still time, indeed. At three-and-twenty, *Catherine* should be Well Married and settled by now." Turning to Kate, she added, "Why you didn't seize the chance to marry Lord Harcourt's heir in your second season, I'll never understand."

Kate's cheeks flushed a deeper shade. "I—that is—" She swallowed.

Ben lowered his port. No matter how he might wish to hear more of this heir—who sounded rather stuffy—Lady Catherine must be diverted from her inquisition. "My lady," he said, his voice deeper with his irritation. "How long can we enjoy the pleasure of your company in Newford?"

Lady Catherine narrowed her eyes at him for a long measure. "You've your grandfather's cheek, Mr. Kimbrell."

"Thank you."

As the aromas of the evening meal wafted in from the adjacent dining room, he didn't miss the grateful look Kate tossed him. Though he was feeling a bit wrung out, he was pleased he'd come.

CHAPTER ELEVEN

THE NIGHT OF the squire's supper arrived, and Bronwyn and Ben had agreed to meet at Kate's home for the short drive to Trevelyan Abbey. There was no sense in the Parker carriage descending the hill only to make the turn and climb it once again.

Kate dressed carefully for the evening. She didn't know if Merryn would attend now that he'd given over the task of designing the sets to Ben, but she wished to look her best. The theater production had taken much of her time of late, and she'd had little with which to think on her matrimonial aims. The thought was a sobering one. With her grandmother's dire criticisms fresh in her mind, she considered the very real possibility that she'd never marry if she didn't put forth a proper effort.

She'd donned a favorite gown of oyster silk. The

neckline was square and perhaps a shade lower than she normally wore while a delicate design of leaves adorned the hem. She lifted a piece of her mother's jewelry—a simple gold chain with a single pearl teardrop—and clasped it round her neck.

A long-suffering sigh sounded behind her, and she eyed her sister's reflection in the glass. Alys lounged along the length of Kate's pale-yellow counterpane, ankles crossed demurely at one end and her head hanging—not so demurely—from the other. Her sister's face was upturned, her unpinned plait bouncing toward the floor as she read from her novel.

"Is it a tale worthy of such heartfelt sighs?" Kate asked as she smoothed a stray curl. Her sister had always had an excess of feeling. While Kate enjoyed an engaging romantic novel, she felt they rarely considered the practicalities of life. Sighs were well and good, but someone must see that the grocer's bill was paid.

Alys lowered her book and spun to sit up. "Oh, Kate. It's the most enchanting story! The Count de Montclair has just defeated the villain and shaken off the chains of a horrid betrothal to sweep the fair Genevieve into his arms. They plan to elope as the clock strikes midnight." At Kate's frown, she marked her place with a ribbon and set the book aside. "Do you not long for such a passion? For a gentleman's merest glance to set your heart aflutter?"

Kate opened her mouth on an automatic denial then snapped it shut again, for what lady didn't long for heart-fluttering glances? She tempered her reply with, "Of course, but there's a difference between the love you read about in novels and the affection that will best serve you in life."

Alys lifted a brow in silent challenge, looking too adult for her years, and Kate continued. "Love is important, certainly, but there are other factors to consider when choosing a husband. Wisdom and good sense can't be overlooked." At her sister's snort of skepticism, she added, "A match founded on mutual admiration and respect will endure far longer than any heart-fluttering sentiment."

"Is that a question or a statement?"

Kate, recognizing that the words had come out weaker than she'd intended, cleared her throat. "It is a statement of fact," she said more firmly. "Just look to any couple whose marriage was founded on practical considerations and mutual compatibility, and you'll see that lasting happiness comes from a steady and prudent regard rather than idealistic fancies."

"Any couple... Like Mr. and Mrs. Pentreath, perhaps? I've never seen a more practical union than that of our solicitor and the resolute Mrs. P.

Why, she must be near to bursting with happiness."

"You're being deliberately obtuse," Kate said. "And disrespectful."

"You've only to look to our own parents to disprove your theory," Alys replied. "By all accounts, they were deliriously happy for having Followed Their Hearts." Alys enunciated the sentence in the style of Lady Catherine and Kate pressed her lips.

She couldn't argue that their parents had enjoyed a love worthy of one of Alys's novels, their mother defying both Lady Catherine and good sense to marry where she wished. But Alys was too young to recall the arguments. Forgotten commitments. Unfulfilled promises. Her father's long absences as he attended lecture after lecture. Kate bit her tongue against the truth as Alys returned to her novel.

Her sister was young and could dream all she wished of counts and villains and midnight elopements. Kate would continue her efforts in Merryn's direction. He was a man of wit and intellect. Of honor and character. What she felt for him was a steady admiration, rather than the heart-fluttering, dizzying heights of passion, but that didn't make it any less genuine. And love would come in time. Surely, it must be easy to love a man like Merryn Kimbrell.

She returned her attention to her preparations for the evening, although the exchange with her sister had left her feeling a bit flat. She ignored her disquiet to lift a green silk ribbon to her dark hair, then one of blue velvet, studying each in their turn in the mirror.

"The blue," Alys said without looking up. Despite their differing perspectives on love, Kate couldn't dispute her sister's natural eye for fashion.

"The blue?" she said. "Do you think so?"

"He most certainly favors the blue."

Kate dropped her hand, the ribbon forgotten. What did Alys know of her hopes regarding Merryn? But more importantly... had her sister observed a corresponding interest on his part?

Alys continued reading as if she'd not just tied Kate's insides into knots. When she offered no further explanation, Kate licked her lips and asked, "How do you know he favors the blue?"

Alys lowered her book with a sigh. "It's easy enough for anyone to see, though I don't think he'd mind if you walked about in curling papers and a burlap sack."

Kate's breath tightened in her chest. "It—it is? That is, he wouldn't?"

Alys snorted and lifted her novel once more. Kate hesitated before passing the blue ribbon to Mary to thread through her curls.

When Kate finally descended the stairs to the front parlor, she found Bronwyn and Ben had already arrived. They were entertaining her grandmother with a tale of one of their cousins' escapades, though *entertaining* was a relative concept to judge by the tight seam of Lady Catherine's lips. Kate's father, seated in a patterned damask chair next to Lady Catherine, had his head down as he perused his latest issue of *The Botanical Register*.

The pair of them would join their party at the squire's supper, her grandmother as an honored guest and her father as escort. While her grandmother saw the outing as a necessity—*it's always good to Be Seen, no matter the society*—her father would sooner have gouged his eyes with a garden trowel. Kate was confident there must have been some form of coercion involved.

She greeted her friends with a quick nod of her head for Ben and a squeeze of Bronwyn's hand. Her friend wore a demure pale pink gown of brushed muslin that brought out the roses in her cheeks. Though the effect was charming, Kate doubted the shy-miss picture she presented would fool anyone for long.

And Ben… well, he fairly took all the air from the room. A tailored black coat was well fitted to his tall form. Beneath it, he wore a pristine white shirt with a starched collar, a simply knotted cravat and a pearl stickpin. His black trousers were impeccably pressed, and a waistcoat of dark grey fooled one into believing him possessed of a quiet elegance.

He wore his dark hair neatly combed, and she suspected a bit of pomade had been employed to tame the curl near his temple. His hard jaw had recently seen the edge of his razor, and she caught the familiar spicy scent of his shaving soap. It made her think of Newford's seaside cliffs—all blooming heather and salty sea. Even when he was away to London, whenever the breeze blew in her window just right, she was reminded of him. Now, his dark blue eyes flashed beneath the thick fringe of his lashes as he greeted her.

Yes, she thought. He was quite handsome and rather grown up, and she told him as much. To her surprise and intrigue, his cheeks colored at her words.

"And you light the room," he murmured as he lifted her hand in his. His gaze took in her form from her hair to the tips of her embroidered slippers, and Kate felt a curious dip in her stomach at his inspection. Although *inspection* wasn't the correct word. It had felt more like a... caress. She swallowed, reminded of one of Alys's heroines, and pushed the thought aside to tease him instead.

"Such pretty manners. Perhaps your time in

London hasn't been wasted after all."

"As you say."

Kate's father looked up from his journal, and it was a moment before his distracted gaze cleared. "Ho, but we make a fine group," he said.

Kate's grandmother eyed her from tip to toe, much as Ben had done, but it felt markedly different. "You'll do, Catherine. Remember, shoulders back, chin up. I believe your squire's son remains Unattached yet." The reminder of her matrimonial aims effectively cleared all thoughts of Ben's handsome good looks from Kate's mind.

Alys, vexed that she wasn't permitted to attend, wisely held her complaint. She said only, "I shall await your return. Here, alone." She ended this declaration with only the merest of sighs, which Kate supposed was a sign, small though it was, of her sister's growing maturity.

"Don't wait up," their father said. "You know the Squire's suppers can last hours"—he scrubbed a hand over his face at this—"and there's no reason to disturb your rest."

Her sister's shoulders slumped before she recalled their grandmother's presence and stoically pulled them back again. Kate took pity on her. "Never fear," she promised as her father led their grandmother from the room. "I shall bore you with all the details later."

She pulled on her gloves—she'd been pleased to find them where they ought to have been—and her sister assisted with the buttons.

As Alys did up the final one, she leaned close to whisper, "Isn't it just as I said?"

Kate sent her a sidelong look, a frown of inquiry tugging her brow.

"He favors the blue."

———

BEN ASSISTED BRONWYN and Kate into the Parker carriage then took the remaining place on the rear-facing seat next to Kate's father. Lady Catherine's full presence took up much of the opposite seat, with Kate and Bronwyn wedged neatly to one side of her.

He'd not been able to miss the warm, barely-there scent of wild roses that drifted up from Kate's hair. Or the slight tremble of her fingers as he'd handed her in. Alys had whispered something in her ear as they were leaving. Her sister's words had caused a frown of confusion to crease Kate's brow for the merest moment before she cleared it. Now, her face had returned to its usual mask of serenity as she gazed out the carriage window. Perhaps her change in mood was only a figment of his imagination. He crossed his arms and studied her profile as the carriage rumbled forward.

"Did you have a chance to begin practicing your lines for the first act?" Bronwyn asked, interrupting his perusal. "Miss Carew has already begun preparing for the second, and I wouldn't want us to fall behind." As she spoke, Bronwyn slid a curious glance toward Kate. It hadn't been his imagination then. Something had upset her, but the devil take him if he knew what it was.

"Aye," he said in reply to Bronwyn's question.

"Oh, that's good," she exclaimed with unflattering surprise. "That's very good."

Kate pulled her attention from the window and smiled. With what looked like a fortifying breath, she said, "The pair of you will make a splendid Beatrice and Benedick. Don't you agree, Papa?"

"To be sure," he replied without conviction, and Ben supposed Parker's mind must still have been on the journal he'd left behind.

"D'you think so?" Bronwyn said. "I hope we're able to capture the spirit of their connection..." Bronwyn carried the conversation as the carriage rolled on to Trevelyan Abbey. Kate remained quiet, interjecting occasional comments for the duration but otherwise content to hear his cousin's soliloquy. He couldn't miss, though, that she eyed him with unusual scrutiny when she thought his attention was elsewhere. He rubbed a hand over his jaw, wondering if he'd left a bit of shaving soap behind.

CHAPTER TWELVE

KATE'S SURPRISE AT Alys's words was eclipsed only by her confusion. Bronwyn continued speaking about the play, and Kate tried to attend the conversation, but her thoughts wouldn't stay in line. Not with Ben seated across from them, as indolent as he was elegant. He filled the space, and she wondered if he'd always done so or if her thoughts made him appear larger.

Then he tossed about one of his crooked grins, his even teeth flashing in the dim light of the carriage lantern. Surely, there was nothing odd about his manner, nothing to indicate he held anything but the friendliest of affections for her. Alys was simply seeing things that weren't there.

She recalled her earlier suspicion that Ben had developed a *tendre* for a lady in London. Even he wasn't so lost to propriety to carry an affection for

Kate while he pined for a love he'd left in London. No, her sister had read too many novels. Alys's youthful imagination had simply run away with her better sense.

Kate had learned long ago not to mistake Ben's familiar manner for anything more than it was—the easy, cheerful demeanor of a friend of long standing. He'd never so much as attempted a kiss after that first spring, and even that was suspect, for he'd denied it. *Don't be silly*, he'd said.

Keeping their association in its proper box in her mind—with the lid firmly pressed—was a path that would serve her well. Ben was a friend and only a friend. There. Her disordered thoughts were reordered once more, and her breath came more easily.

The carriage rolled to a stop in the squire's circular gravel drive. The door was opened, and her father and grandmother went down. Ben stepped from the carriage next to assist Bronwyn. When he reached for Kate, his hand was solid and warm through the thin cloth of her gloves, and his eyes searched hers. She was almost certain there was a weight to his gaze that hadn't been there before. Her stomach took another swooping dip toward her toes, and she chided herself for her foolishness. She'd dismissed Alys's words on the strength of her sister's vivid imagination, but whose imagination had broken its tether now?

She pulled in a bracing breath of the evening air and moved to join their party on the steps of Trevelyan Abbey. The twelfth century structure rose high above the surrounding landscape, its weathered battlements and sturdy stone towers silhouetted against the approaching twilight. Lanterns glowed behind colorful stained-glass windows, and the ruins of a centuries-old cloister reposed next to the squire's carefully manicured lawns. Bronwyn had often regaled her with childhood tales of playing with the Carew children among the Abbey's ruins or hiding in its many not-so-secret passages.

The ladies turned their cloaks over to a servant, and their group was met by the squire and his wife before moving to an expansive drawing room. After they were announced, her grandmother urged her father to a position near the top of the room, the better for guests to pay their respects. Several members of the play's ensemble had already gathered, and Bronwyn and Ben were quickly drawn into their conversation.

Mrs. Pentreath stood rigidly alongside several matrons from the Ladies' Society. Her husband said something (which the lady ignored) before taking himself off to circulate the room. Kate watched as Mrs. Pentreath frowned her disapproval at his back. She fought a sigh of irritation for annoying sisters and turned her thoughts instead to the other guests.

Her eyes quickly sought out the tallest of them, landing on Ben's cousin Gavin as well as the squire's son. Bronwyn hadn't been certain if Merryn meant to join the party—*My brother rarely tells me his schedule*—but it quickly became apparent that he wasn't in attendance. Kate's disappointment wasn't as acute as it ought to have been, for all the thought she'd given her attire for the evening.

Many of her neighbors were in attendance as well as several of Newford's marriage-minded visitors. Kate joined a number of conversations, discussing roses with Mrs. Tretheway and inquiring of Mr. Clifton's latest bakery confection. In time, the squire's son joined her with his sister and Gavin Kimbrell. Kate accepted a glass of Madeira as Mr. Carew said, "Miss Parker, you're just the soul of reason we need to resolve a dispute."

"I'm not certain I can settle your matter, but I'm happy to offer my opinion if I can."

"Fans," Miss Carew said without preamble.

"I beg your pardon?"

"Fans. Or rather, the use of a lady's fan to gain a gentleman's attention. That is our topic."

"I see," Kate said, although she wasn't certain she did. "And you're debating the propriety of such a gesture?"

"Heavens," Miss Carew said as she unfurled a

fan of delicate pierced ivory. "We left propriety at the door. We're debating the *intent* of such gestures. I contend that a glance directed at a gentleman from behind a lady's fan conveys a wealth of information without the exchange of a single word."

The constable frowned at this. "'Tis unreasonable to expect a gentleman to discern a lady's thoughts from a mere plying of her fan," he said. "Who's to say she's not simply become overheated? Perhaps she's hoping the gentleman will procure her a lemonade."

"With her eyes? Only the most obtuse of gentlemen would fail to interpret such a glance. Do you not agree, Miss Parker?"

Miss Carew awaited Kate's agreement while Gavin Kimbrell looked increasingly uncomfortable with the turn of the conversation. Kate was certain there was more at play here than a discussion of ladies' accessories, and she felt as if she balanced atop one of the sea-slicked boulders at Copper Cove.

"Well... while I appreciate the need for subtlety," she began, "we ladies are complex creatures, are we not? I'm afraid I must yield Mr. Kimbrell's point that the nuances of a lady's thoughts may be lost to such a mode of communication."

"Well said," Mr. Carew exclaimed as the tension in Gavin's frame eased a fraction. "The Foreign Office could use your talents, Miss Parker."

"I—I suppose you may be right," Miss Carew said a bit breathlessly. "I confess, I've never thought of it that way, but it must require a discerning mind to grasp such subtleties. To be sure, not everyone possesses such keenness of thought, and we mustn't fault the gentlemen for desiring a simpler approach."

Kate, admirably, refrained from wincing as Miss Carew fired a cannon through her carefully crafted peace treaty. Gavin frowned and excused himself to procure the lady a lemonade, "my limited faculties not being equal to anything more than that simple task."

When Mr. Carew's attention was claimed by another guest, his sister leaned toward Kate. "Do you truly think it's as simple as all that when a gentleman fails to acknowledge a lady's efforts? I only ask on behalf of a friend, of course."

Miss Carew's brows were pitched to a point, her worry evident. Kate knew something of the lady's frustration. She considered her reply, and gentle phrases of reassurance came to mind. But she thought Miss Carew, who waited so intently for her response, wished for more than platitudes. For her friend, of course.

You always know the proper thing to say. Though far from accurate, Ben's earlier assurance gave her the courage to offer gently, "Well, I suppose it *is* possible the gentleman simply remains unaware of the lady's intent. Or… his silence may come from a desire to spare the lady's feelings. In such situations, your friend might be better served to seek her happiness elsewhere. She will surely find a gentleman on whom her affection is not wasted."

The advice caused a niggling sense of unease to settle on Kate. Like a splinter, it itched beneath the skin, and she didn't have the faintest idea how to pull it out. Miss Carew's lips pulled into a smile, and Kate felt her disappointment keenly.

Bronwyn, who'd rejoined them with Mr. Carew, interjected, "Well, I for one believe this flirtation business would be heaps easier if young ladies were permitted to be more direct."

Mr. Carew laughed. "Miss Kimbrell, that's as likely as men driving a coach and four to the moon. It would upset the natural order."

"Quite so," his sister agreed softly.

"But just imagine," Bronwyn urged, "a lady telling a gentleman outright of her interest. Why, we could dispense with all this"—she waved a negligent hand in the air—"back-and-forthness."

Her words carried the pointed tone of a friend offering unsolicited advice, and Kate cast her a questioning glance. Bronwyn merely lifted her brows as she sipped her sherry, but any further conversation ended with the sound of footsteps approaching the drawing room. More guests had arrived, and everyone waited to see who it would be.

The squire's servant opened the double doors to reveal Mrs. Matthews and her companion. Both ladies were fetching in their evening attire, and Mrs. Matthews had shed her widow's colors to don a gown of rich, port-wine silk. She was a vision of elegance and sophistication—the rare orchid to Kate's common rose. Her gown's graceful neckline flirted with the tricky edge between modest and daring—certainly, it provided a bit more interest than Kate's own bodice, which she had once thought rather bold.

The lady's coppery locks had been gathered to frame her face with artful refinement, and elbow-length satin gloves and a lace fan completed her ensemble. A fan! Did she anticipate the cool spring night would turn overly warm, or did she hope to employ the accessory to some other end?

And then, immediately following the ladies, came Merryn. It was impossible to tell if he'd accompanied Mrs. Matthews or merely arrived as the ladies had. Kate found her smile as he made his rounds of the room.

———

BEN FROWNED AS Merryn entered the drawing room on the heels of Mrs. Matthews' very fine slippers.

While everyone watched the new arrivals, Ben watched Kate. She was magnificent, softly elegant in both looks and manner, with not a single sign to betray her thoughts. He didn't think any but he noticed her interest in Merryn, so adept was she at hiding it. But he prided himself on his ability to read her moods, and her dismay was writ clearly enough for him to see. Dismay for which he felt partially — mostly? — responsible. He'd been the one to encourage Merryn in the direction of the widow, after all.

Merryn reached Kate's group, and she smiled, eyes bright as he gave an elegant bow over her hand. Ben's coat felt too tight, the conversation of his neighbors muffled beneath the pounding in his head. He pulled in a shallow breath and considered the hours-long supper ahead of him. He eyed the door. Could he make his excuses and go? It would be a long walk back down the hill. Then the squire's servant announced supper, putting an end to that notion before he could make his escape.

The company, four and twenty in total, made a merry group as they prepared to enter the dining room. In Newford, where the gentlemen always outnumbered the ladies, there was often little formality to the procession, but Mrs. Carew must have been overdone to have both Lady Catherine *and* the marriage-minded visitors in attendance. She sorted them all very properly in order of rank and honor, and Ben found himself near the back of the line. His sleeve was occupied by Miss Brightbury, a twittering miss he understood was newly arrived from… somewhere. Hampshire perhaps. Merryn, who was his equal in family if not in fact, stood near the front with Mrs. Matthews, and Kate walked in with Mr. Carew.

They settled into their places at the squire's long, linen-draped dining table, Ben at one end between Miss Brightbury and another young lady, Merryn at the other between Mrs. Matthews and Kate. Miss Brightbury spoke enthusiastically of her home in Wiltshire—not Hampshire, as it turned out. She was engaging if a bit exhausting, and he flirted dutifully with both ladies at his side, though his eyes strayed more than once to the other end of the table.

Merryn divided his attentions between Kate and Mrs. Matthews, as was proper, and Kate wore a slight flush that betrayed her pleasure. They made a fetching couple, he admitted to himself, and Kate *would* make a fine hostess as Merryn expanded his business ventures.

The footmen poured more wine, and he pulled his eyes from Kate to take in the room's appointments. It was a long-standing habit, this study of his surroundings, and had led to mountains of sketches in his desk where he'd embellished or improved upon a space. There was little to improve upon in the Abbey's dining room, though.

It was symmetrical and nicely proportioned to accommodate the squire's large dining table. Rich wooden panels covered the walls while exquisitely detailed plasterwork adorned the lofty ceiling. The gracefully arched sash windows with their slender mullions hinted at a recent renovation, done to great profit by Merryn's firm.

He turned from his study of the millwork and met Kate's assessing gaze. She'd been watching him—studying him much as he studied the room. His neck heated beneath her scrutiny. She gave him a soft smile before returning her attention to Merryn. His cousin murmured something that caused her smile to grow, and Ben forced his grip on the delicate stem of his wine glass to ease.

The fish was brought out, and as the footmen came round, the squire lifted his glass. Speaking from his position at the foot of the table, he said, "I'm pleased the Ladies' Society has reached an accord on the matter of our theater's first performance. I wish you all well in your efforts to bring a bit of refinement to Newford in what I expect will be the first of many entertaining diversions to come."

"Hear!" Mr. Clifton said as Mrs. Pentreath's lips flattened.

The conversations about the table then turned to

the preparations for the play. "How do the sets progress?" Mrs. Clifton asked. The question had been directed at Kate, who lowered her fork to reply. "They do very well, Mrs. Clifton. I think you'll be pleased with what Mr. Kimbrell and I have planned."

"Ah, yes," Mr. Carew said. "I heard Kimbrell was to do the sets." He motioned down the table and said to Ben, "Should we expect another Kimbrell's Folly to grace the stage?"

Ben tossed the man one of his careless grins as laughter rippled through the guests. Carew's words had been spoken in the spirit of good fun, and Ben couldn't fault the question. Before he could offer a proper retort, though, Kate stepped into the breach.

"Ben has prepared some rather inspiring drawings," she assured them. "His vision is extraordinary."

"Aye," Mr. Clifton said, "but 'taint his *vision* that be in doubt."

Kate's eyes narrowed the tiniest bit, and Ben was charmed by her loyalty even as he questioned its wisdom. "But surely, Mr. Kimbrell's castle is far more arresting than any finished piece could be. It carries the tragic air of ruin. One can easily imagine the romance and intrigues that might have passed behind its walls. It's genius, truly." *Too brown, Kate.* "I've always thought it must be more difficult to

137

craft a compelling bit of history than to build a shiny, new thing. Wouldn't you agree?"

She looked at Mr. Clifton and Mr. Carew in turn, but neither could gainsay her without appearing ungentlemanly. Lady Catherine's lips were flat at this stout defense of his folly, but Kate studiously avoided her grandmother's gaze. She wasn't finished, it seemed. "Ben has an eye for detail that is unmatched. The sets for this production will be nothing short of extraordinary. Certainly, no play in Truro has ever been done so well."

Her color was high above the squared neckline of her gown and her eyes shone. Ben wanted to urge her to stop talking, but in truth, she was rather magnificent. He almost believed the nonsense she was spouting, and warmth spread through his chest as she tossed him a tiny, lip-biting smile.

But then Merryn spoke, drawing the conversation, and Kate's attention, to other matters.

CHAPTER THIRTEEN

Offices of Mr. William Wilkins, Architect
No. 10 Bedford Square
London

8 May 1820

Mr. Benedick Kimbrell
Newford

Dear Sir,

I trust this letter finds you safely returned to Cornwall. I write to express my appreciation for your recent visits to London and our engaging discussions, particularly those pertaining to my expansion endeavors at Lord Falmouth's esteemed Tregothnan.

As a gentleman deeply committed to the field of architecture, I continue to admire your observations, and I hold your capabilities in high regard. I wish to take this opportunity to renew my offer, namely, that proposal for you to join me in London as a junior associate.

As we discussed, this arrangement will afford you the opportunity to further your studies. I don't pretend the benefit is all to your side, as I would welcome the opportunity to mentor a gentleman who shares a similar passion for this delightful and complex discipline.

I kindly request your decision at your earliest convenience so we might begin the necessary arrangements. I eagerly anticipate your favorable response.

Yours etc.,
Mr. William Wilkins
Architect

———

"HAVE YOU RECEIVED upsetting news?" Kate asked.

Ben looked up, surprised to see her outside his cousin's small post office, brows knit charmingly above her nose. That he'd not even noticed her approach said much for his distraction. He hastily refolded Wilkins' letter and tucked it into his coat.

"Not at all," he said with a smile, though it felt put on. Kate was a vision in pale green, her cheeks flushed from the warmth of the spring day. She carried a basket of flowers, and he took it from her before extending his arm.

"You're away to visit Mr. Simmons then? Shall I accompany you?"

———

KATE COULDN'T DENY the relief that eased her shoulders when Ben offered to escort her to Mr. Simmons' cottage. The old man's temper, which was known to be gruff at the best of times, had grown sharper of late. She supposed that was to be expected, given the hardships he'd faced. Mr. Simmons had lost his eldest son, Diggory, some years back and more recently, his wife. And now Jago, his youngest, was often away to Truro, getting up to all sorts of mischief, to hear the constable tell it.

As she and Ben neared the end of the high street, they encountered Ben's brother Alfie and his cousin Jory. The men tipped their hats pleasantly and eyed the basket of flowers at Ben's side with poorly concealed amusement. They kept their thoughts to themselves though, and once they'd passed, Kate grinned at Ben. "It would appear your secret is out."

"Aye, so 'tis," he grumbled, but his blue eyes flashed with humor.

"I wonder that they didn't say anything. I wouldn't have thought them eager to let an opportunity to tease you pass."

He shifted her basket in his hand. "Twasn't polite restraint that held their tongues. Only yesterday, I caught the pair of them at Morwenna's, holding piles of hair ribbons for their brides."

"Ah, it's to be a mutual blackmailing," she said. "Their silence for yours."

"'Twill serve us all."

Kate didn't point out the fallacy in this logic — that carrying Kate's basket of flowers could hardly be on a level with husbands assisting their wives. She and Ben weren't even courting, after all, much less wed to one another. But she enjoyed this solicitous, gentlemanly side of him as much as she did his company, so she kept her thoughts to herself and allowed him to carry her basket.

They descended lower into the valley and soon found the entrance to Mr. Simmons' lane. Ben lowered his arm to the small of Kate's back to assist her around a puddle. It wasn't more than a tiny dip in the path that she could well have negotiated herself, but she couldn't fault his manners. She was dismayed, though, by the tiny, corresponding dip in her stomach as it fluttered warmly at his kindness. Would that her stomach could proceed in life with as much caution as her head, but it seemed everything below her neck—stomach, heart, all of it—was determined to ignore her better sense.

They rounded the final hedge, and Mr. Simmons' home appeared. No smoke curled from the chimney, and dark windows stared out at them unseeing. One side of the roof sagged, and several slates had come loose to lie broken on the ground beneath the eaves. Thick weeds covered what had once been a tidy yard while bits of pink and purple peeped through the dense growth—intrepid remnants of the few flowers that had once brightened the place.

An angry dog—black and dark-eyed and missing part of one ear—barked at them from the end of a fraying rope. Ben hesitated, a frown creasing his brow as he took in the state of the man's property. Kate shared his dismay. She'd described it to Ben as tired, but it was worse than that. Mr. Simmons' home had lost its soul.

Ben glanced at her basket of flowers, and she knew what he was thinking. It would take far more than a few rosebuds to cheer the place. She swallowed, gathered her resolve and knocked on the door. The dog's barking persisted, but there was no response from within.

After a long minute, Ben reached past her and knocked more forcefully. "Simmons!" he called.

Finally, the door jerked open, and a wave of stale air soured with old sweat and gin rolled over them. Mr. Simmons, unshaven, bleary-eyed and well into his sixth decade, peered out. Stained clothing hung from his angular frame.

"What?" he barked. Then, seeing Kate beside Ben, he lowered his voice and took a step back. "Aye, 'tis only ye then."

"Good afternoon, Mr. Simmons," she said. "I've brought fresh flowers for you as well as some loaves of Mr. Clifton's bread."

"Tol' ye afore, us don't need yer charity or yer posies. 'Tis only Nell and me now." Nell, on hearing her name, stopped barking, but she continued to watch Kate and Ben with dark-eyed suspicion from the end of her lead. Brushing aside Mr. Simmons' gruffness, Kate stepped inside.

The Simmons cottage had once been a neat and well-made home, built by Simmons' own hand back when Diggory had been alive to assist him. Now, though, an empty hearth left the space cold and dim. Neglect was evident in the parlor's peeling paper and floorboards that hadn't seen a broom in an age. Water dripped from the ceiling into buckets as if the house had suffered a mortal wound.

A sparse kitchen lay beyond the parlor, and Kate went through without invitation. The scene there was no better, and she frowned at the iron pot rusting on its hook. An empty bottle of spirits lay on its side to puddle the floor. Even the mice had been neglectful, leaving a bit of molded cheese where it sat atop the small chopping table.

Kate placed the bread in Mr. Simmons' bare larder then found an old cloth to wipe the mess on the floor. Little else could be done without soap and pots and pots of hot water. Returning to the parlor, she replaced the dead flowers on the small dining table with fresh blooms from her basket. As she worked, she held up a one-sided conversation. "Mrs. Simmons always enjoyed roses, but I recall she had a special place in her heart for the bluebells. Do you remember how she enjoyed watching the fields grow purple with them?"

The lines of Mr. Simmons' face softened a bit at the mention of his wife before assembling again. She pressed on. "Did you know bluebells symbolize enduring affection? I suppose it's on account of their ability to bloom year after year in the same place."

There was no response to this fascinating bit, so she tried another tack. "I imagine you've heard there's to be a play at the new theater. The Ladies' Society is settled on one of Mr. Shakespeare's comedies, and Mr. Kimbrell has designed the loveliest set. Aren't you a carpenter yourself, Mr. Simmons? I imagine the two of you must hold a shared interest in..." She cast about and finished with a vague, "builderly things."

Ben looked vaguely alarmed by this suggestion and not at all inclined to take up his end of the conversation. He'd found a position near the door, feet braced and arms crossed against the shadows. He was ridiculously tall in the low space. Kate fell into silence, straightening things and arranging flowers until she was satisfied. The more she moved, the less she felt the heart-withering effects of Mr. Simmons' glower.

When she finished, she waved a hand at the room behind her. "It appears the kitchen could use some tending. Would you like me to send one of our girls to put things to rights?" The Parker housemaids would leave without notice if they knew she was offering them up for such a task, but Mr. Simmons, as he'd done for the past months, promptly refused her overture.

"I can 'andle me own business." He pulled his bent form up in an effort to intimidate, his thinning hair nearly brushing the low ceiling.

She refused to shrink, saying only, "Of course, I didn't mean to imply otherwise. But should you ever desire—"

"I won't." Despite her best intentions, she did take a tiny step back then.

The chill in the cottage sent a shiver across her shoulders. She didn't know how he could bear it. With the merest hesitation, she said, "Perhaps we could tend your fire—"

"'Me own business' includes me own fire."

"Simmons," Ben growled, and Kate was surprised by the authority in his voice. "'Tis easy enough to see where Jago comes by his manners."

Ben's words—or perhaps the strong, low tone in which he'd said them—captured Mr. Simmons' attention. Emotion shadowed his face before he wiped it clean with a wide palm and lowered himself in slow, jerky movements onto a chair in the small parlor. He withdrew into his own thoughts, his awareness of them folding by degrees like a worn letter.

Kate cast an uncertain glance at Ben, who frowned. Then without a word, he knelt at the hearth to add a log to the cold grate.

———

BEN DUSTED ASH from his hands as the fire cracked and popped in Simmons' firebox. He waited while Kate satisfied herself that she'd done all she could for the man and his house. When she finished, she pressed one of Simmons' bony hands between her smaller ones, promising to return soon.

The old man remained on his parlor chair, gruff and unyielding as she went through the door. Ben studied him for a long moment before following her, his steps heavy on the dirty wooden planching. Before he reached the sunlight, though, Simmons surprised him with an uneven laugh.

"I see ye're still trailin' the Parker lass's skirts."

Ben hesitated before pressing the door closed. He turned back to face Simmons, arms crossed and feet braced. He didn't bother with a denial, or even one of his careless grins. "Why d'you care?" he asked.

"Don't leave things undone such as ye did wit' yer folly." Simmons cleared his throat, the craggy planes of his face shifting before he added, "Regret, 'tis a poor companion."

Then, having exhausted his wisdom, Simmons turned his gaze to the hearth. In the flickering light of the new fire, his dissipation was more apparent, his cheeks florid from too much drink. The older man's pain was so evident it thickened the air, despite his efforts to hide it behind his sharp-edged demeanor. And, like a bolt from a summer storm, the stark truth streaked across Ben's awareness, sending a chill along his neck.

He and Simmons weren't so very different.

Oh, Ben was younger, it was true. And cleaner.

A sight more handsome—and it wasn't vanity but reality to acknowledge such a thing. But while Simmons concealed his pain behind his bottle and bluster, Ben shielded his heart with cavalier smiles. They were the both of them... cowards. And who was foolish enough to say Simmons hadn't once been young and clean and handsome himself? Ben drew a long inhale as the roar of his blood filled his ears.

He stared at the back of his hand, unable to look on his future self. A long moment passed before he said, "I'll keep your words under advisement." He hardly recognized the voice for his own.

Simmons erupted with a harsh, mirthless laugh that ended on a cough. "Go on," he scoffed with a nod toward the door, so Ben did just that.

The sun, warm and bright in a cloudless sky, was a welcome relief to the gloom of Simmons' cottage. Kate waited for him some distance along the path, and the sight of her beneath the light-dappled trees eased the tightness in his chest.

"Why d'you do it?" he asked once he'd rejoined her.

She didn't ask what he meant but said, "Did you not see him? He'll wither and die like his flowers if no one tends to him."

"And d'you not think that's precisely what he wishes? His spirit has given up on this life." As the words left his lips, his voice caught. He—Ben—

had not surrendered. He and Simmons might share some similarities, but Ben's heart was not so hopeless as that. He cleared his throat as Kate turned her face up to him.

"Are we simply to pretend we don't see his suffering?"

He sighed. "Of course not, but Simmons is a man grown. Only he can choose his path."

"There's nothing to say we can't help him clear the brambles from it."

Ben rubbed the back of his neck. It was on the edge of his tongue to agree—it was a kindness to extend aid to a man who didn't want it. But instead, he added gently, "You can't change a heart's course, no matter how you might wish otherwise."

Her gaze remained fixed, fittingly so, on the path ahead of them. But then she blinked—once, twice— and he stopped.

"Kate."

She turned, and her brown eyes shimmered, bright and dark at once and endlessly deep. Her unfallen tears nearly undid him. Extending his hand, he allowed his little finger to brush hers before he dropped it.

She smiled, a valiant effort to be sure, though the tiny freckle at the corner of her lip trembled with the effort. With a silent curse for propriety, he reached out once more and pulled her to him. To his surprise, she came easily, allowing him to fold her in his arms. He didn't ask the reason for her tears—he didn't think he could bear it if she wept for Merryn—but he held her to him.

———

MESSY SOBS THREATENED her composure. Kate held them in, but just barely, forcing even breaths and stealing comfort from the smooth press of Ben's hands at her back. From the hard warmth of his chest beneath her cheek. She teetered between Slightly Undone and A Shocking Display. It wouldn't have taken more than a word from him to nudge her headlong over the cliff. As if he sensed this, he remained silent, supportive but allowing her space to collect herself.

With one last bracing inhale, she lifted her head. "My apologies. I fear I've dampened your shirtfront."

He pulled his head back to look at her, his lips tipping up on one corner. "'Tis a poor shirtfront that can't withstand a bit of dampening."

She chuckled and stepped back, acutely aware of the loss of his warmth. "I'm not certain what came over me," she said and immediately felt contrition for the lie.

You can't change a heart's course. Did that not sum it up rather nicely? She wished to marry and, though Merryn would make an acceptable match, her heart simply wasn't engaged in the effort. No amount of persuasion could move it.

Meanwhile, her friend had no qualms about carrying himself off to London without a thought for those he left behind. Honesty compelled her to admit—silently at least—that she'd been waiting long years for him to finish stealing his kiss. But, like his castle, he'd abandoned the endeavor all too soon, if he'd ever meant to do it at all.

Just imagine, a lady telling a gentleman outright of her interest. Bronwyn's words from the night of the squire's supper came to her unbidden. If only things were as simple as her friend made them sound, but Kate couldn't imagine anything worse than confessing her feelings aloud, only to find Ben didn't return them. Why, they'd never be easy in one another's company again.

How had things become so tangled? More importantly, would she ever see them untangled? And that question set her eyes to stinging again, for she didn't think she could bear much more wanting. She was so weary of it.

He got them walking again, and they soon arrived at the lane above her home. Her father was just visible inside his glasshouse, and the valley rolled and stretched beyond. Ben's castle stood on the opposite ridge, tucked charmingly behind its thick shroud of wild roses. This was one of her favorite prospects, and she didn't argue when Ben slowed their steps.

A muscle ticked in his jaw as he stared at the structure. He seemed… sad, although that was such a simple word for the complex expression on his face.

"Why did you speak out for the folly?" he asked. "At the squire's supper."

She considered her answer before replying. "Well, I suppose it's because Mr. Clifton makes a fine mince pie, but he has no imagination when it comes to your castle. They should all be made to see its beauty."

He gave her a soft smile—not one of his meant-to-charm grins, but a real smile that pulled at the corners of his eyes. "Kate, you're the only person who persists in calling it a castle."

Her heart pinched at the bleakness in his tone. No matter what propriety said, no matter what—or whom—he'd left in London, he was her friend, and she couldn't bear his sadness. He deserved the same measure of comfort that he'd extended to her.

With only a small hesitation, she reached for his hand. They stood like that for a time, his hand warm in hers. Finally, because she wished to know more of what lay behind his easy grin, she said, "While I do think it's the prettiest castle about, I wonder… if you're displeased with it, why did you never finish it?"

———

BEN PRESSED KATE'S fingers, relishing that single point of contact. She awaited his reply, and a smile came easily to his lips, as did a glib response. *Rome wasn't built in a day*, perhaps, or *Without a princess in the tower, it seemed a futile effort*. Old habits, he supposed.

Then he thought of Simmons' lonely misery, and he checked his instinctive reply. Instead, he gave her the truth. "'Tis *because* I'm displeased with it that I didn't finish. The angle of the roof isn't right, nor the scale or proportion of the tower. And you, Kate, deserve nothing less than perfection."

A frown pulled at her slim dark brows. He watched her gather her courage, and the strength of her gaze when she turned it on him made his breath catch.

"It may not be perfect in the lines or the angles or whatever it is that concerns you," she said softly. "But it was a gift from your heart that I will always cherish."

Her eyes were steady on his, and the connection between them lit like the flare of a match, its glow warm and intimate and illuminating in the fragile moment before it dimmed. And then, like a match, the moment was extinguished, and he thought he must have imagined it.

"If people were buildings," she continued with a thoughtful smile, "I think you would be your castle."

Her words startled a laugh from him. "Rough and incomplete?"

"Charming and capricious. Concealed from those who would know it and..." Her eyes narrowed as she studied him, searching for the words. "...perfectly imperfect, I should think." She gave a short nod of approval. "Yes, I like that."

Perfectly imperfect. His breath caught at the phrase. It was how he'd always thought of that spring so many years before, the season when they'd met just before everything changed for him. She waited for his reaction, so he quirked a brow at her to say, "Charming, I'll not dispute, but perfectly imperfect? That sounds like an apology."

She shook her head in ready denial. "Perfection is suspect. I find imperfection much more... trustworthy. Hopeful, even, for there's always possibility."

He wasn't willing to concede such logic. Some things were so imperfect, so flawed, they could never be recovered, but he saw the appeal in what she said. It was there in the bright anticipation of something more, something greater than what had gone before.

But his curiosity must be sated. "And you, Kate?" he said. "If you were a building, which would you be?"

"Oh no," she said with a laugh. "You must make the assessment. What do you think?"

He rubbed his jaw in consideration. His thoughts went first to her father's glasshouse with its profusion of beautiful growing things within. The structure was both simple and elegant, but he swiftly dismissed it as a suitable reflection of Kate. She was much stronger than a house of glass and not half so delicate as he'd once thought. Certainly, her inner workings were less transparent.

He considered their parish church—for modesty and virtue—and the squire's dining room at Trevelyan Abbey, which carried its own pleasing balance of symmetry and depth.

Kate chewed her lip as she waited, and it came to him. "Our balcony," he said.

She stilled. "You do realize the balcony is not a *building*?"

"I do, but it fits." She prompted him with a lift of her brows. "There will be a lovely garden on one side," he said, "and the refinement of our villa on t'other. A bit of earth and elegance to match your spirit." She smiled at that and he continued. "'Twill be graceful, if I can manage it, and it's... unexpected."

"Unexpected?"

"Just when I think I've sorted all your angles, you turn to reveal a new scene more enchanting than the last."

"Oh," she said, drawing the syllable out. "I quite like the sound of that, even if it does come from a charming and capricious castle." Below them, her father left his glasshouse and strode across the gardens toward the house. Kate pulled her hand from Ben's and turned to go, pausing to say over her shoulder, "As a point of clarification, I never expected—I never *wanted* perfect."

Ben's breath, when he found it again, was sharp like the gasp from an unexpected plunge into the cold sea. It was the stuttering sort of reflex one experiences when faced with something wholly unexpected.

When he'd given Kate the simple truth of his castle folly, he'd expected polite reassurances. He'd expected soft words of comfort to ease his doubts. He'd not expected the fragile implication that she'd wanted *something* from him. Warmth filled him as he gathered her words close. *I never wanted perfect.* Unexpected, indeed.

CHAPTER FOURTEEN

O VER THE NEXT week, Kate's time was consumed with preparations for the play. In addition to the sets, she'd taken on the costumes with Morwenna and Bronwyn, and she spent a good many hours organizing the actors for their rehearsals. She felt the smallest bit of guilt for leaving Alys to their grandmother, but then she need only remember her Sunday gloves to absolve herself. Or more properly, she need only remember the parish children's home, which would benefit from a successful production.

The pace of activity was a welcome diversion from her thoughts, which raced round a track that started and ended with the strength of Ben's arms as he'd held her on the lane above Mr. Simmons' cottage. Just when her cheeks cooled from that, she'd recall that he had stopped building his castle because it wasn't perfect. For her. It wasn't perfect *for her.*

He'd not abandoned it because he'd grown bored or become distracted by something else. His words, and the earnest way in which he'd delivered them, suggested he must have felt *something* for her beyond the affection of one friend for another, even while her head argued that if such were the case, surely he would have acted on his feelings by now. When such lowering thoughts showed themselves, she quickly stuffed them beneath *You deserve nothing less than perfection.* Which in turn brought forth the perfection of his hands against her back.

And so would begin the round all over again. The constant looping of her thoughts was enough to give a body a headache. She finished sewing a line of buttons onto the sleeve of Leonato's coat only to find she'd sewn the sleeve to her skirt. Bronwyn, on seeing her dilemma, released an unladylike snort and passed the scissors.

Despite her hours at the theater, she'd spent few of them in Ben's company. He rehearsed his scenes in the mornings before shifting his attention to the sets. Certainly, there'd been no furthering of their discussion, although she could feel his gaze on her at times. The heat of it fairly set her blood to simmering.

Many of Newford's marriage-minded visitors had made a habit of arriving at the theater in the late morning hours to watch the actors rehearse their scenes. They would take their places on the front benches, twittering like so many sparrows on a branch whenever the gentlemen read their lines. One particular miss was often given to *sighing*, much like Alys with one of her novels. Kate recognized her as the energetic young lady from Wiltshire who'd walked into the squire's supper with Ben.

Now, though, rehearsals for the day were nearly ended and the ladies had gone. A relative calm settled about the theater. Many of the candles had been extinguished, save the ones closest to the stage. The resulting shadows darkened the entry and hugged the benches. She could hear Ben moving about behind the stage where he'd been working for some time, and she wondered how his balcony progressed.

She'd had a few peeks over the past days, but it seemed little more than a rough frame so far, all angles and timbers and little that resembled an Italian villa. She eased her uncertainty with thoughts of his castle, which was a remarkable display of his talent. She firmly pushed aside the fact that it was also unfinished.

Miss Carew, having completed her scenes for the day, prepared to leave with her maid. "The play is coming along rather nicely, don't you think?"

"'Tis indeed," Bronwyn agreed.

Kate lowered the scissors and folded her hands over the mess that lay before her. "It's just as I predicted, Miss Carew. Never has Hero been played with such grace and energy, I think." The praise came more easily this time. Miss Carew still delivered her lines with enthusiasm, but the breathy quality of them had eased a bit. The change must have been apparent to Gavin Kimbrell as well, for he seemed to have relaxed into his role to deliver his own lines with more assurance.

"We wouldn't be nearly as prepared without your gentle herding of our flock," Miss Carew said as she pulled on her gloves. Then, lowering her voice in an aside, she added, "Let's only hope you've found as much success with the sets as you have with the cast." As if to punctuate her statement, hammering resumed from the back of the theater.

Kate's answering smile felt a bit tight. Why could no one see beyond Ben's castle? "The sets will be wondrous," she said. "You'll see."

Miss Carew left them, and the theater doors opened to admit golden sunlight and Mrs. Matthews. Both were equally bright. The lady was dressed today in a cornflower-blue walking dress and a chipped bonnet that she wore *rakishly*.

Kate had never thought to apply the word to ladies' fashion, but there was no other way to describe the smartness of the widow's attire. She looked as if she'd just left her fine London townhouse to drive herself about the park.

Mrs. Matthews had taken to joining them for tea at the Feather on the occasional afternoon. *Keep your enemies close*, Bronwyn had said. Judging by the ease with which Bronwyn greeted the lady, Kate wondered if she herself had ever been on Bronwyn's list of enemies and been unaware of the fact.

Regardless, she couldn't deny Mrs. Matthews had an odd sort of charm about her—a compelling force that drew ladies and gentlemen alike. People couldn't help but enjoy her company, and to Kate's relief, the lady's sophisticated manner didn't cause nearly the anxiety it once had. That Kate had all but abandoned her thoughts in Merryn's direction was a fact she chose not to over-contemplate.

"Good afternoon, ladies," the widow said when she reached them. "Goodness, Miss Parker, have you sewn a coat to your skirt?" She laughed, though the sound wasn't unpleasant. "I abhor mending and can't tell you how many times I've done the same. Socks seem to be my particular enemy."

Kate smiled, though she had trouble picturing the elegant lady bent over her mending, much less making such a silly mistake. Somehow, the thought of Mrs. Matthews near anything so common as a sock seemed ludicrous. "I'm afraid I was woolgathering," she explained as she resumed snipping threads.

"Well, once you've sorted it, we can have a nice tea at the Feather if you're not otherwise engaged. Mrs. Teague has some raspberry tarts, fresh from the oven. She's agreed to set some aside, far from the gentlemen's notice."

Bronwyn laughed. "You're learning our ways and our secrets. The gentlemen need not know she bakes up twice as many as they think."

Kate considered the sounds coming from behind the stage. She really ought to meet with Ben to ensure he didn't require assistance. Perhaps they could review the schedule once more and the remaining tasks to be completed. Or they might— she stopped her thoughts. There was nothing to be gained by fibbing to herself. She wished to meet with Ben, and that was that. She'd missed him over the last week.

"As much as I appreciate the invitation and Wynne's tea," she said, "I've still a few things to complete here."

Mrs. Matthews twisted her lips in a frown of disappointment. "Very well, but I shall ask Mrs. Teague to reserve a tart for you," she promised. "And what of you, Miss Kimbrell?"

"Oh, I always make time for tea," Bronwyn assured her. "It won't take me but a moment to tidy up. Perhaps you can help me return these costumes to Morwenna's shop."

"Excellent!" Mrs. Matthews occupied herself with collecting the garments, folding each and replacing them in the box they'd brought from Morwenna's.

Bronwyn set aside her sewing to ask Kate softly, "Are you certain you don't wish to join us?"

Kate hesitated before responding. If she'd always thought of Ben as her dear friend, then Bronwyn was her *best* friend. And yet, she'd not said anything of the thoughts racing round her mind this past week. They were too fragile, like spun sugar. Releasing them would surely leave a brittle mess.

Swallowing, she said only, "I wish to see what assistance I can lend to Ben." At Bronwyn's arch look, which seemed a bit too *knowing*, she added, "It's only that there's much to do still, and time is short."

Bronwyn pulled her lips to one side in a poorly concealed smile. "Aye, time is short. Lots to do. 'Tis probably a wise course," she said, which was less reassuring than it ought to have been.

Kate knew a tiny bit of worry over the propriety of it all—of remaining behind with Ben once the others had gone—but she was well past the first blush. She and Ben had often enjoyed one another's company with not a brow raised. They'd walked together countless times. As children, they'd enjoyed picnics near her home, and later, tea in the

Parkers' front parlor. To be fair, one of their relations had often been present to give the appearance of respectability. To be truthful, the task had often fallen to Bronwyn, who'd never taken it too seriously.

Now, Bronwyn angled her head to give Kate a considering look as she tied her bonnet strings. "Something is different," she said. "You are different."

Kate merely lifted her brows at this.

"You've more vigor about you. A liveliness to your eyes that wasn't there before."

"Heavens, Bronwyn," Kate said. "Have I been dull?"

"Of course not, only..." Bronwyn didn't finish the thought but added with a smile, "Well. If you should change your mind about the tea, come join us at the Feather."

Kate nodded her agreement. The hammering had stopped, and she turned to see Ben on the stage, in conversation with Mrs. Matthews. His hair was in disarray as if he'd run a hand through it more than once. He'd long since removed his coat to roll his shirtsleeves, and stubble shadowed his jaw. Kate's breath caught. He was so very... very masculine. And then Mrs. Matthews shifted, and her rakish bonnet blocked Kate's view.

She gave the scissors a final snip, perhaps a little

too vigorously as now she had a hole in her favorite dress. She ignored it and thrust Leonato's coat aside.

"Mr. Kimbrell," she said, hurrying to the stage with her best smile. The pair of them looked up from their conversation, and she scrambled for what to say next. "Ah... might I beg a moment of your time regarding the... um... the sets?"

The look he gave her was blank for the briefest of moments. Then, eyeing Mrs. Matthews in her fine blue walking dress, he grinned. "Aye, the sets. D'you have a change you'd like to make? Or, per'aps you've merely something 'charming and capricious' you wish to discuss?" This last was said with a wink.

Kate's blush and frown were immediate and simultaneous. Mrs. Matthews looked at them as if they were daft as doorknobs. To Kate's relief, Bronwyn soon collected her and the ladies left, leaving the theater in silence save for the thumping of Kate's heart.

Ben lifted a box of supplies from one of the benches, and she didn't miss the way the movement showed his shoulders to advantage. "I hesitate to comment on a lady's attire," he said, "but you've a hole in your skirts." With a grin bordering on irreverent, he turned and went through the door that led behind the stage.

Kate blew a puff of air through her lips. They'd

seen the last of the cast for the day, so she extinguished some of the candles. The resulting shadows darkened the entry and hugged the benches, though the stage remained lit. It wasn't long before the sound of Ben's hammer echoed in the stillness once more, and she made her way behind the stage. She'd begged a moment of his time, after all.

Unlike the tidy front of the theater with its neat rows of benches, the back was a study in organized chaos. Two small rooms were set aside for the performers to change their costumes, but beyond that, the space was given over to the building and storage of the sets. Large timbers were stacked on one side while saws, buckets of nails and jars of paint lined another wall. Over it all lay the combined scents of woody turpentine and fresh sawdust.

Ben stood with his back to her, hammer in hand next to a large wooden frame. She must have made a sound because he lowered his arm and turned. Heavens, he'd abandoned his neckcloth. Kate had a glimpse of masculine chest above the narrow opening of his shirt and vest, and her stomach dipped alarmingly.

"What d'you think?" he asked.

She pulled her eyes from his chest, up the hard column of his throat and past the line of his stubbled jaw to find him watching her. Amusement lit his gaze. She'd been caught staring, and heat rose to fill her cheeks. Friends or not, she was certain that tantalizing glimpse—and the resulting swoop of her belly—were less than proper.

"What do I think?" she repeated numbly. The room was much too close, and she glanced about for a window she might open.

"The balcony."

"Oh! Of course. I..." He moved aside to reveal the structure he'd been hammering. Since she'd seen it last, he'd added a floor and balustrade. Walls—the interior of the villa, she presumed—leaned against the theater's back wall, waiting to be attached. His set was taking shape. She offered up a silent prayer of gratitude. "Well, it's starting to look like a balcony, I suppose," she said inanely. What in heaven's name had happened to her tongue?

He grinned, and she had the distinct impression he was laughing at her. She waited for him to make a teasing comment about her sudden loss of intellect, but he merely nodded at the villa's walls. "Aye. A few more days ought to see the interior finished, and I can begin work on the garden side."

"That's good." At his silence, she pressed, "Isn't that good?"

He rubbed the back of his neck, and the action pulled at the open collar of his shirt. She forced her eyes to remain on his face. "Aye, 'tis good," he agreed, but his tone didn't instill confidence.

She frowned, forgetting her heated cheeks. Though she had no concerns regarding his talents, she didn't think she could bear it if Newford had reason—another reason—to doubt him. "If time is a concern," she said, "we can bring on extra hands. We'll invite the townspeople to assist, and I'm certain your brothers and cousins—"

"I prefer to manage the work myself."

"Of course, but—"

The low pitch of his brow halted her words, but before either of them could continue, a crash sounded from the front of the theater. It was followed by a loud and inventive curse which Kate was certain had not been intended for delicate ears. Her eyes widened, and she rushed from the room, Ben following close behind.

They returned to the front to find Mr. Simmons' lanky form sprawled in the shadows amongst several upended benches.

"Mr. Simmons?" she said in surprise.

"Why 'aven't ye lit any bleddy candles?" he asked gruffly, his words slurred. He tried vainly to extricate himself from the benches, and she hurried forward to assist. He waved her off with a growl and a hammer which, despite his fall, he held fast in his grip.

"Mr. Simmons," she said once more, "why have you come?"

Ben snorted without humor. "He's brought my extra hands, 'twould seem."

———

BEN HAD BEEN taking more pleasure than he ought to have from Kate's discomfort. It was clear and not a little encouraging that she found the open collar of his shirt intriguing. That the theater was emptied of guests and cast hadn't missed his notice, either. But—and here he sighed—now he must deal with Simmons.

Even from a distance, he could tell the man's breath was stale and heavy with the odor of spirits. Ben strode forward and righted several of the benches, but he didn't offer his hand. He'd no wish to lose a finger on the sharp edges of Simmons' pride.

"'Eard ye were buildin' something. Brought me 'ammer," Simmons said as he lifted the tool.

"Go home, Simmons," Ben urged in a low whisper that neared a growl.

Simmons lowered the hammer, eyeing Ben with remarkable irritation for one so bleary-eyed.

"Don't make me toss you out in front of Miss Parker," Ben pressed in a voice for Simmons' ears only. "I'll not hesitate on your account, but I've no wish to distress the lady."

He thought Simmons might argue, but after a bit

more blustering, the older man finally gained his feet. His gait was unsteady, to no one's surprise, as he lurched toward the entry. Ben strode forward to aid his exit, opening both doors before Simmons could pull them from their hinges.

Ben saw the man as far as the surgery next door, where Dr. Rowe would grant him the use of one of his beds. He returned to find Kate righting the remaining benches, and he bent to help her.

"It's sad," she said, "to think he was once a skilled carpenter. One of the best, to hear the townspeople tell it."

"Aye. He and my uncle were acquainted long before my uncle's accident." He swallowed and cleared his throat before continuing. "My uncle once told me Simmons wields—wielded—his hammer like an artist's brush."

Kate was silent for a long moment before she said, "Perhaps he just needs to find his purpose again." She looked about the theater, considering. "Do you think he could—"

"No."

"But everyone needs a purpose," she pushed.

"Then invite him to help in your garden." Her lips twisted at this flippancy, and the delightful crease that formed when she was irritated made an appearance. Seeing it was almost worth her displeasure.

"I don't think Mr. Simmons' purpose lies in

gardening," she said primly.

"You've seen him. He's half seas over. D'you think his 'purpose' lies in anything but his bottle?"

"Perhaps not," she said thoughtfully. "But there's still a good bit to be done on the sets. Perhaps you could give him the odd task here and there. Idle hands being what they are, I imagine that could do much to bolster a man's spirits."

Ben snorted. "His 'spirits' need no bolstering." She frowned at this, and though he enjoyed her irritation, he'd never wish to truly upset her. He softened his voice to add, "Kate, a man like Simmons can't be fixed with mere industry. The odd task isn't enough to settle the disquiet in his soul. He needs to have success and accomplishment in the work, but he'll not find it in his condition."

She nodded though he wasn't sure she believed him. Then Kate drew her head back, and he had the uncomfortable feeling that she... studied him. Her brows pulled low, her rich brown eyes dark and assessing. He thought to return to his work behind the stage, but he was unable to pull away.

"First you talk of perfection, and now you speak of success and accomplishment," she said with a tinge of accusation. "For all your carefree ways, Ben Kimbrell, you harbor *ambition*."

"I do not." His denial was a reflex, like a sneeze to pepper.

"You do," she retorted triumphantly. "How have I not seen it before? Oh," she said, pressing her hands to her lips. "I have been the worst of friends."

Ben scrubbed a hand over his eyes. This conversation had grown much too heavy. He was wondering how he might distract her again with his chest when the doors to the theater flew open once more and reprieve arrived in the form of his brothers. Kate sent him a look that said she was not abandoning their discussion, and he turned to Daniel and Matthew with more of a welcome than they were used to having from him.

"Bronwyn sent us," Daniel explained as he hefted a basket onto one of the benches.

Surprised, Ben opened the top to investigate. His brows lifted at the sight of warm bread and roast chicken and a pair of paper-wrapped, tart-shaped parcels. There were jars of cider, wedges of cheese and fresh cherries. His stomach growled, as it had been some hours since he'd eaten. He marveled that his cousin—who wasn't normally prone to fits of thoughtfulness—had packed two of everything.

"Did she send any of Wynne's tarts?" Matthew asked eagerly.

"Aye," Ben said as he continued rummaging in the basket.

"Can we have one?"

"No."

"Did she send lemonade? What about some of the Feather's biscuits?"

Daniel frowned at his brother. "Bronwyn said we're not to linger, in case—"

Matthew's elbow connected with his brother's rib, eliciting a low grunt.

A folded paper lay tucked along the side of the basket. Ben slid it out and found Bronwyn's hastily scratched note. *Wynne sends her "wooing basket" and assures me it rose to the occasion for Jory.*

With the slow-dawning awareness of the very obtuse, Ben finally discerned his cousin's intent. He hastily tucked the paper into his pocket. Bronwyn must suspect the direction of his feelings. Had Kate said something to her—hinted at a change in her affections perhaps?

His brothers waited as if they expected a coin for their troubles, and Ben indicated the doors with a terse jerk of his head. When Matthew only wiggled his brows in Kate's direction, Ben made a note to advise them later on the fine art of discretion, though he feared any counsel he might offer would be lost.

For now, though, he thrust the paper-wrapped parcels at them. "Take the tarts," he said.

They didn't give him a chance to change his mind.

When they'd gone, Ben turned to Kate, and his

mouth dried. Her color was high though a smile curved her lips. She'd likely guessed Bronwyn's purpose in sending the basket—Kate wasn't nearly so slow about these things as he was. Pleasantly surprised that his voice didn't break, he said, "Bronwyn has sent more than enough for the both of us. If you're not otherwise engaged, would you like to take a late luncheon?" Before she could refuse, he added, "'Twill be like one of our picnics in the meadow."

CHAPTER FIFTEEN

K ATE'S GAZE FELL once more to the opening of
Ben's shirt before she swiftly brought it up
again. Despite his claim, luncheon with him
now—alone in the theater—would be *nothing* like
their picnics in the meadow. They weren't children
any longer.

She felt the pounding of her heart clear to her
fingertips as she said, "I'm not otherwise engaged."
The moment felt significant, as if she were saying
much more than the words themselves.

His face relaxed into one of his easy grins. "I'll
just wash up," he said. "I won't be but a moment."

He left her, and she lifted the lid on the basket.
Bronwyn had sent a cloth, which she unfolded on
the stage. By the time she finished setting out the
food, Ben had returned. His face and hands were
free of sawdust, his hair finger-combed back from

his forehead though he hadn't been able to tame the curl at his temple. She was disappointed to see he'd fastened his collar and retied his neckcloth, though it appeared as if he'd rushed the effort. She bit the corner of her lip against a smile.

He waited for her to take her seat at the edge of the stage before he sat. The theater was dim beyond the pool of candlelight that ringed the stage. She could barely see the last row of benches at the back. The shadows wrapped them like a soft wool blanket, creating a hushed intimacy that suddenly had her tongue in knots. Perhaps she should have lit some of the candles again.

She poured cider into a mug and handed it to him, but her words were slow to come. Finally, taking inspiration from the cold beverage, she said, "How does your brother's cidery venture fare?"

He lifted his mug and swirled the contents. "'Tis early still, but it seems to be a rousing success," he replied. "I don't think Alfie knew there was so much to learn about pippins, but he's borne it without complaint, as that's his way. Wynne purchased much of his first batch for the Feather, and I understand he's already found buyers in Truro and Falmouth for next season's barrels."

Kate had enjoyed cider before, but she was more accustomed to wine and champagne. She lifted her cup and took a tentative sip. It was crisp, with the earthy aroma of apples and spices. The fermented blend wrinkled her nose before the light sweet-sour taste emerged. "Why, it tastes like sunshine," she said with surprise.

"Alfie will be pleased to hear it. Per'aps he can fetch a better price for sunshine," he said as he saluted her with his cup.

She smiled her reply and took another sip. The silence lengthened around them as they sorted Bronwyn's offering onto their plates, and she wondered that such awkwardness had grown between them.

"What novel is Alys reading these days?" he finally asked.

Gratitude filled her for the question, and her tension eased. "I'm not certain of the title, but there's a count and a dastardly villain, of course. And I believe there's to be a midnight elopement soon. It seems the most dreadfully contrived plot, but you know Alys has always loved such dramatics."

Mischief lit Ben's eyes as he leaned close. "Why do you suppose elopements must always happen at midnight?" he asked. "Has anyone ever eloped over luncheon or tea?"

She laughed. "I don't think a luncheon elopement carries the same weight of romance. The midnight hour is much more mysterious and alluring."

He made a sound of agreement then, casting her a look through his lashes, he said softly, "I find luncheon to be inspiring in its own right." His gaze remained steady on hers, tightening the breath in her chest.

"I—yes." She was abysmal at this flirting business, if that's what they were doing.

"But what of you?" he asked, releasing her. "D'you find the notion of a midnight elopement romantic?" He wiggled his brows above his grin, and she was relieved to know that, despite her awareness of his intriguing chest, he was still just Ben.

"An elopement is a reckless disregard of the proprieties, so of course it's romantic," she said with a laugh. "But I can't imagine such measures would ever be necessary in my own life. Elopements are for improper matches, after all."

"Ah. We know you would never do anything improper." His words, though teasing, held the suggestion of a challenge.

She tried to imagine doing anything so bold as eloping with Merryn Kimbrell, but the notion was, well, ludicrous. Any courting, if it had ever developed between them, would have been very properly done, with formal addresses paid to her father, et cetera. She'd never have given a thought to anything so rash or imprudent. Ben, on the other hand, could very well tempt her to impropriety. The thought sent butterflies tumbling through her stomach.

"And yet, I'm here," she replied, surprised and not a little pleased by her boldness. He tipped his head in approval, and she returned the question to him. "What of you—do you foresee a midnight elopement in your future?"

He snorted a laugh that had her smiling again. "No. As you say, elopements are for improper matches. If I marry, the lady will be very proper indeed."

A piece of cheese lodged in Kate's throat, and she took another sip of her cider. "If?" she said when she'd recovered.

"Aye."

"Are you uncertain, then, if you'll marry?" She'd never imagined him married—he'd always been, quite simply, Ben, her friend without a past or a future, with family and friends but none that were his alone. The thought that he might never make a family of his own caused a sad, uncomfortable weight to settle in her stomach.

"To be sure, nothing in this life is certain," he said philosophically.

"But everyone marries." She considered her own situation and added, "Eventually."

"And I hope to as well," he admitted, "but I'll not marry without love."

She opened her mouth to say she'd never taken him for such a romantic, then she stopped. Ben was the very definition of a romantic soul. From his fairy-tale castle on the ridge outside her window to the alluring design of his garden balcony to his astute understanding of poor Mr. Simmons' heart, no other gentleman of her acquaintance could claim such a poet's spirit.

His gaze was down, fixed on his long fingers as he turned a cherry stem in his hand. A shock of dark hair hung low over his brow, and she was struck with such a rush of affection for him that it stole her breath.

He looked up, and his deep blue gaze studied her for a long beat. "I—" he began. His jaw tightened as he pressed his lips. She waited, heart thumping a hurried pace, until he surprised her with, "D'you know Jory once planned an elopement?"

"Jory!" she exclaimed.

"Aye."

"Is Anna aware?" she asked on a whisper.

"O' course. 'Twas Anna he meant to elope with."

"Oh, tell me," she urged. She crossed her ankles and nibbled a piece of bread as he told her of Jory and Anna's first engagement five years before, which had not gone as either of them had planned.

Their conversation came more readily then. They

spoke easily of simple things. She told him her plans to introduce new roses to the southwest corner of the garden, and he shared an amusing encounter he'd had with a chimney sweep in London. After, they chewed in silence for a time, but it was a comfortable quiet, the sort shared between friends.

Kate recalled their earlier, interrupted discussion regarding Ben's ambition. If they were truly friends, she thought she should know more of his hopes and dreams.

"What do you want from this life, Ben?" she asked softly. He frowned, and she bumped his arm with hers. "It's only me, and you know I won't tell a soul." At the suspicious quirk of his brow, she added, "Even Bronwyn."

He smiled at that, but finally he pulled a paper from his pocket and extended it to her. She took it slowly. It was a letter and as she read, her mouth fell open. "This Mr. Wilkins—he wishes to mentor you."

"Aye."

"But how? Why?"

Ben pulled in a long breath. "I corresponded with him last year regarding his work at Tregothnan. He shared some of the challenges he'd encountered, and I offered my thoughts. They weren't but trifling matters, to be sure, but my holidays in London—they've been at Wilkins' invitation."

London. He'd not gone to court a lady. She

stared at him for a long beat. He'd been... studying architecture. She could hardly credit how much lighter she felt, weightless even. Architecture—Ben!

"But this is wonderful! Your family must be proud." The expression on his face shifted, and she knew. "You haven't told them."

"Merryn and my father know the reason for my travels, but no one is aware of this letter. 'Til now, that is." It was so like Ben to hold himself back. Her insides went squishy to think he'd trusted her with his secret, even as she puzzled over his reticence.

"But why haven't you said anything? Surely, you must prepare to go soon." Even as she said the words, the lightness in her stomach turned to lead. She didn't know if she was ready for life in Newford without Ben. Her mouth had gone dry and she swallowed.

"I've not decided if I'll go. 'Twould only complicate matters to tell others then decide against it." *Much as it's doing now,* his expression said.

"But why," she began softly, "why would you not wish to go?"

"I want to." His eyes were dark and intense with a passion she'd rarely seen in him. He paused and collected his words then started again. "I want to design and build and create, but 'tis as if my boots are full of ballast. I can't move. Neither forward nor back, up nor down."

She considered his words, uncertain how to respond. Finally, she said, "I think we're all of us precisely where we wish to be at each moment in time. We choose, from the choices laid before us, that which is the least objectionable or the most pleasing." He frowned, and she couldn't say she blamed him. It was a poor translation of her thoughts. Shifting on the blanket, she tried again. "What concerns do you have about London?"

He was quiet for so long she didn't think he would answer. Then he released a breath and said simply, "Expectations." She prompted him with her silence until he added, "If I go, there will be expectations."

"And in Newford...?"

"There are none." He rubbed a hand over his face at this admission, but Kate felt like the moon had emerged from behind the trees. Expectations. Success. Accomplishment.

"This is about perfection again, is it not? You fear"—he frowned so she amended—"you are *concerned* you won't find it. Well, you know how I feel about that." Their hands rested beside one another on the blanket, fingers barely touching. She moved hers the merest inch until their fingers twined together. She marveled at the strength and capability in his hands. It was in his spirit as well. Could he not see it?

"You think I should go."

"I think—" Kate stopped and pulled in a breath. No matter how she would miss him if he left, she couldn't deny the enthusiasm that lit his eyes when he spoke of building. "I think you should consider there will always be expectations—*yours*. You can't avoid them, no matter where you are."

CHAPTER SIXTEEN

KATE'S HAND WAS warm on Ben's—a steady anchor for the thoughts and emotions that ricocheted through him. His insides felt as if they'd been scraped raw. Her words were full of good sense, but he'd not have expected less. She'd given him much to think on, and he told her so. But their impromptu luncheon had grown heavier than he'd intended. He grinned in an effort to lighten things a bit and returned to something she'd said earlier.

"You chose to take luncheon with a friend," he reminded her. "'Twas the least objectionable choice or the most pleasing?"

Her response was delightfully swift. "The most pleasing, of course."

"I'm relieved to hear it, though I'm curious to know what you measured such a weighty decision against."

"Tea with Bronwyn."

"Ah," he said with an exaggerated sigh. "Not much of a choice at all then."

"There were to have been raspberry tarts."

He laughed. She always knew just the thing to tease the heaviness from his heart.

She sat close to him on the stage, her hip touching his. Bronwyn's basket and the remains of their meal lay on the blanket behind them—when had they moved so close to one another? She watched him, her dark eyes an intriguing mix of candlelight and shadow, her face angled in perfect kiss position. What would she do if he leaned forward and touched his lips to hers? Would she be surprised? Without a doubt. She might scold him for his impertinence, though he couldn't forget the warmth of her gaze on his chest. Or would she return his kiss? Oh, hell, now his heart was racing, and she must surely hear it.

He'd flirted with any number of ladies over the years, but never had he suffered such uncertainty. He leaned closer, no more than the merest half an inch. Kate's soft rose scent was warm and inviting. It lifted and swirled from her hair, drawing him closer. Or had she moved? He thought she might have. Her cheeks were pink—delightfully so—and his uncertainty eased a bit to know she wasn't unaffected by their nearness. She licked her top lip and Ben's heart skipped before jumping into a full gallop.

Then the theater doors flew open, the sound crashing-loud in the stillness. The pair of them sprung apart as if they'd been doused with January water. If Daniel and Matthew had returned... But it was Merryn.

Ben's neck heated with a guilty flush as his cousin strode down the dimly lit aisle. Ben was meant to be building the sets, yet here he sat amidst the remains of a bacchanalian feast. A stretch, perhaps, but Bronwyn's basket had been well filled.

He helped Kate to stand. She refused to meet his eye, watching as his cousin neared. Merryn stopped before the stage and took in the blanket and the remains of their meal. His cousin wasn't overly dense and Kate still wore a charming blush, so Merryn probably had a fair notion of what he'd interrupted. He maintained a polite expression, though, and greeted them both with a pleasant, "Good afternoon."

Kate dipped a brief nod and returned Merryn's greeting with a too-bright smile that didn't quite reach her eyes. "Good afternoon," she said.

Ben waited while they exchanged idle pleasantries about the weather and the squire's supper. Kate stood awkwardly, hands clasped behind her back as they spoke, and Ben frowned at her manner. Had he been mistaken to think her affections had shifted? Did she still have hopes in Merryn's direction? His stomach turned uncomfortably, threatening Bronwyn's luncheon.

When Kate and Merryn had exhausted all the usual topics, she said, "You'll wish to see how the sets progress. I expect you'll be pleased with what Ben's completed so far."

"Aye," Merryn said with a glance that included Ben. "He's provided reports, of course, but I thought to see this balcony marvel for myself."

Ben frowned at his cousin's good-natured teasing but motioned to the door that led behind the stage. "'Tis through there," he said.

As Merryn strode ahead, Ben stepped from the stage then turned to assist Kate. She pulled her hands from behind her back, and he was surprised to see she held his letter. She'd been hiding it all this time, keeping it from Merryn's view. Was *that* what accounted for her awkward stance? She pressed the paper into his hand, and he couldn't help but notice how her smile reached her eyes now. His stomach righted itself as he tucked his letter away.

He led the way to the balcony and wondered what his cousin would think. Would he worry the sets wouldn't be finished in time? Would he doubt Ben's ability to see the task through to the end? He'd arrived as Ben was enjoying a leisurely meal. It was entirely possible Merryn would regret having given such an important task to his devil-may-care cousin. Though Ben might claim otherwise, his cousin's opinion mattered.

But that was nothing to his own expectations for the work. Kate, in her quiet wisdom, had been right about that.

As Merryn inspected the balcony, Ben described how he planned to fashion two sets out of one through the use of a rotating platform. His cousin nodded through it all, one hand stroking his jaw as he listened to Ben's explanation. He asked the odd question here and there about mechanics and how, precisely, Ben would install the set on the stage, but otherwise he remained silent. Kate watched from the side, and Ben thought she appeared as anxious as he felt.

"We'll install the balcony at week's end," he said in response to one of Merryn's questions. "There are scenes that must be rehearsed in the villa as well as the gardens."

"I'll admit I thought you might be further along with the construction by now."

"I've had some issues getting the proportions right, but 'twill be done."

Merryn's eyes narrowed a bit as he studied Ben. He didn't say as much, but it was clear he was thinking of Kimbrell's Folly. To Ben's surprise, he said only, "'Tis good. And a fair bit more appealing than slate work, I imagine."

Ben let go a slow breath. "Aye."

As Merryn turned to go, Kate leaned close to Ben. "'Tis good," she whispered in near perfect imitation of his cousin. He almost kissed her right there, but she squeezed his hand before following Merryn back to the stage.

With one last glance at the remains of their picnic, his cousin turned to Kate. "Miss Parker, may I escort you to the Feather? Bronwyn will welcome your company on the walk home."

Ben rubbed a hand along the back of his neck. The impropriety of their luncheon was clear, as was Merryn's intent to resolve said impropriety. Kate opened and closed her mouth then, with a short nod, she agreed. "I'll just collect my gloves."

As she did so, Merryn leaned toward Ben. "Careful, Cousin," he said softly. "Know your heart before you break hers."

———

KATE FOLDED HER hands before her as she walked alongside Merryn. They met Mrs. Clifton as the lady left her husband's bakery. Kate nodded politely while Merryn tipped his hat. The late afternoon sun had striped Newford's high street in variegated shadows, which suited Kate's mood. Weeks before, she'd have been pleased beyond measure to share such a moment with Merryn. She'd have walked slowly, if only to lengthen the opportunity, but now, she found herself thinking only of Ben, and the kiss they'd almost shared. (She was certain of it. Very nearly.) She shoved her thoughts aside. Without the sun's warming rays, there was no excuse for her color.

"It promises to be a fine evening," Merryn began, hands clasped behind his back, gaze aimed forward. The line of his jaw was firm above his crisp neckcloth.

"Yes," she replied. And then, "You're pleased with the sets?"

"Aye." Merryn cleared his throat and added, "I never doubted they'd be finely done," which sent him up a notch in her estimation.

"Ben will finish in time, if that is your worry." She wondered, if Merryn did hold such a concern, why he hadn't offered any assistance. Surely, he must have carpenters who could lend a hand to the effort. Men who were a sight steadier than Mr. Simmons. Merryn's next words, though, preempted any further thought along those lines.

"My cousin has long had a stick caught in his wheel, so to speak. Ever since my father—well. I hoped that his recent travels might have loosened it, but..." He lifted one shoulder but didn't give voice to the rest of his thought.

Kate's hands tightened at her waist. She wouldn't betray Ben's confidence by revealing his letter, but she couldn't help saying, "Ben told me you're aware of the nature of his travels to London."

Merryn cast her a sideways glance. "Are *you*?"

She nodded.

Relief eased Merryn's features but only a bit. "I'm pleased he's confided in you, but I worry he won't find his way. First London and now his balcony... Though 'tis a fine piece of work, is it enough to move him forward? I don't know." At Kate's frown, he added, "My apologies. 'Tis much too heavy a conversation for a walk to the Feather."

"It's not that, it's only—I'm uncertain if you mean to offer a warning or seek reassurance."

"Which d'you think?"

Kate swallowed, certain her answer was important, though how, she couldn't say. Opting for reassurance, she said earnestly, "There's more to Ben than anyone sees. He'll sort it."

Merryn's smile was swift. It might have melted her heart if the organ wasn't already taken. "Your certainty is reassuring. Hold fast to it, Miss Parker. I see more of the old Ben when he's with you," he said. "He's easier. His smile is truer. That's a lot to put on a person, I know."

They'd arrived at the Feather by now. As Merryn held the door, she said, "Think nothing of it, Mr. Kimbrell. You care for him, as do" — the words emerged more softly than she'd intended, so she tried again — "as do I."

CHAPTER SEVENTEEN

BRONWYN WAS PACING the stage when Kate arrived at the theater the next morning. This was odd on two counts, as her friend wasn't an early riser, nor was she given to morning exercise.

"Oh, Kate," Bronwyn said breathlessly, "thank the heavens you're here." She stopped her pacing and jumped from the stage. The urgency in her friend's voice sent Kate's heart plummeting to her half-boots.

"Why, what's happened?" Her thoughts immediately went to Ben. Had he taken ill? Was he injured? Her gaze shot to the door that led to the back of the stage before she reconsidered. Bronwyn's concern was more likely for Merryn. He was her brother, after all. "Is it Merryn?" she asked.

"Oh, 'tis nothing like that," Bronwyn assured her

as she moved toward the exit. "But Morwenna's been positively overrun with new orders from the incomers. It seems they must have new gowns for every outing, and 'twill be a wonder if she's able to finish the costumes for the play. I'm going there now to lend my assistance."

Kate sagged in relief, though she wondered why Morwenna hadn't said anything of her concerns the previous day. Her confusion grew when Bronwyn added, "I'm afraid you'll have to step in and practice my lines with Ben."

"But that doesn't make any sense. Why don't I assist Morwenna so you can rehearse with Ben? Don't you need to practice as well?"

Bronwyn stopped and turned. Crossing her arms, she said softly, "I'm sorry Kate, but my stitches are a fair bit straighter than yours."

"My stitches are straight!" Kate whispered back with indignation, though there was no one about to hear them.

"And," Bronwyn added with a twist of the knife, "I don't sew sleeves to my skirts. Trust me, Kate, 'twill be better all around this way."

Kate's suspicions rose when Bronwyn refused to meet her gaze. "Wait!" she called as her friend made her escape. Bronwyn paused, one foot out the door. Instead of pressing her, though, Kate found herself asking, "Which scenes are we to practice?"

Bronwyn smiled. "'Tis only one—the final scene. And don't let my cousin leave out any important bits," she admonished. "He has a tendency to improvise."

———

THE BRASS BELL above Morwenna's dress shop chimed merrily when Bronwyn entered, but she frowned to find the space empty. She was about to leave and seek her cousin at the Feather when she heard laughter from one of the back rooms. Turning, she strode in that direction to find Wynne suffering Morwenna's measuring tape. Jory's new bride, Anna, was there as well, fingering a length of pale pink silk on one of Morwenna's worktables.

Wynne's rounded belly was barely visible beneath the loose cotton of her shift, but her bodice was arguably more fitted than it had been just a week before. "How many more times d'you think you'll have to let out my seams?" she asked Morwenna with what could only be irritation.

"Several more, I suspect," Morwenna murmured around a mouthful of pins.

Anna dropped the pink silk and turned to face the pair. She was considerably more petite than Wynne and considerably more advanced in her pregnancy. As a consequence, she'd grown quite spherical in recent weeks. It was a fact of which she seemed well aware as she grumbled, "At least you don't resemble a ripe blueberry."

Bronwyn had to admit that Anna, dressed in a gown of brushed blue muslin, did somewhat resemble a plump fruit. She hid her smile and dropped quietly into a chair along the wall. None of her female relations had been forthcoming with details about their married lives, their pregnancies or anything remotely interesting. With luck, this day might prove more enlightening than she'd expected.

"My mother said she had to abandon corsets altogether when she neared her confinements," Wynne said. "She didn't leave our house for weeks."

"Aye," Morwenna said. "To be sure, the discomforts of carrying a babe are not for the faint of heart."

"And let us not forget the cravings," Anna added. "I've developed a liking for spiced ginger biscuits, and I don't even like ginger, but that's nothing to what my friend Mary Riverton writes about. She's grown fond of pickled onions, of all things. Gads. I'm certain her husband will be pleased when that passes."

"If her husband is anything like Roddie, I don't think he'll allow such an inconvenience to dampen his ardor," Wynne replied.

"You're right," Anna conceded. "I grow round as a barrel and Jory only grows… fonder." The three of them laughed as if this made even a lick of sense.

Bronwyn couldn't hold her silence. "What on earth does that mean?" she asked, at which point they sobered on finding a maiden in the room. It was truly maddening.

Morwenna poked her head around Wynne's shoulder to say, "I thought you would be rehearsing with Ben."

Bronwyn sighed, resigned to learning nothing more of interest. But heavens, pickled onions! She suppressed a shudder and replied, "Kate's reading my lines today. I've come to assist you with the costumes."

Morwenna's brow creased in confusion. "But I don't need help. They're nearly finished, in fact."

"Well, let me sew a button, at least, or attach a bit of lace to something." Bronwyn might have exaggerated a bit to Kate when she'd explained the urgency of her mission, and she'd no wish for her words to become an outright lie.

Morwenna shrugged. "The soldiers' coats are just over there. I suppose there's no harm in adding an extra button or two if you feel so inclined." The bell at the front of the shop rang, and Morwenna left them to tend to her customer.

Bronwyn stood and went to the shelf with the

soldiers' coats. She rummaged about until she found a pot of silver buttons. As she took up needle and thread, Wynne took up the conversation. "Kate's standing in for you as Beatrice?"

"She is." Bronwyn bit her lip against a smile. This organizing business was turning out far better than she would have thought. Daniel and Matthew had returned to the Feather the previous evening to report that Kate and Ben had seemed in pleasant accord with one another. And when Kate had joined her later, she'd been quiet. That wasn't so unusual, but Kate had been quietly *contemplative*. To be sure, there was something on her friend's mind.

"Which scenes are they practicing?" Wynne asked.

"The final one." Bronwyn glanced up from the button in time to see her cousin's lips twitch.

"'Tis unfortunate there's to be no kissing," Wynne said. "'Twould make for a more... authentic... performance, but I recall you said Mrs. P was rather emphatic about it."

"Aye," Bronwyn confirmed as Morwenna returned. She paused in tying off her thread to say, "But now that you mention it, I may have forgotten to pass that bit of instruction along."

"You may wish to rectify that," Morwenna said with a press of her lips. "I just spoke with Mrs. P. She's joining several of the matrons at the theater to check the play's progress."

Bronwyn stilled for the merest moment before tossing the coat from her lap. The needle pricked her thumb, but that discomfort was nothing to her stomach's acrobatics as she hurried from Morwenna's shop.

CHAPTER EIGHTEEN

UNDER NO CIRCUMSTANCES was Ben going to kiss his cousin. It was true he didn't have sisters, but Bronwyn was as near to one as he imagined a female might be. Kissing her was out of the question. He marked his place in Mr. Shakespeare's play and tossed it onto his bedside table as Matthew and Daniel stormed his room. He grudgingly moved his feet, and they made their usual noises as they jostled for position at the end of his bed. Lord, his brothers had grown another two inches overnight.

"Are you practicing for the play?" Daniel asked as he took up Ben's worn copy.

"Aye." Ben was grateful for the diversion, even if it must come from his brothers.

His gratitude was short lived, though, as Matthew asked, "How was your luncheon with

Miss Parker?" His brother was striving for a casual manner, but the light of curiosity in his eyes betrayed him.

Ben narrowed his gaze. "'Twas fine."

"Did you share a *confection*?"

Daniel's odd emphasis pulled Ben's brows into a low V. "No," he said slowly. "If you'll recall, I gave Wynne's raspberry tarts to the pair of you."

"He means a *confection*," Matthew offered unhelpfully. His tone suggested he couldn't quite credit his older brother's ignorance. At Ben's continued frown of confusion, Matthew rolled his eyes and said, "A kiss?"

Ben snorted. "'Tis that what you're calling it? A confection?"

"Aye," Matthew said defensively. "Didn't your tutor cover euphemisms? They're helpful when you don't wish to refer to something outright in polite company. As in, I *shared a confection* with Alys Parker just last week."

Ben coughed. At least his youngest brothers weren't hiring housekeepers, but he didn't think Kate would like to know her sister was sharing confections with anyone. And there was Miss Alys's heart to consider as well.

He pulled an audible breath through his nose before saying, "To be sure, an occasional, discreet sharing of confections"—he mentally scrubbed a palm over his face—"can be pleasant, but don't forget, 'tis your responsibility as a gentleman to have a care for the lady's heart and her reputation."

"Aye." Matthew's expression was surprisingly thoughtful, and Ben wondered if he'd actually said something worth their consideration.

Daniel, who'd been thumbing the pages of the play, straightened, lip curled in distaste. "Did you know Benedick and Beatrice share a kiss in the final scene? Bronwyn's pleasant enough as far as cousins go, but I imagine kissing her would be akin to kissing a sister."

Matthew's expression was no less horrified. "You've our condolences, Brother."

Ben groaned and snatched the play from Daniel's hands before rolling off the bed. He took his coat from its hook and thrust his arms into the sleeves.

"Where are you away to?" Matthew asked.

"To tell Bronwyn to find another Benedick." In truth, it was too late for such a change, but there was no reason they couldn't take a little poetic license with the Bard's words. He couldn't even credit that Mrs. P would allow a kiss at all. Perhaps he might convince Bronwyn a brotherly peck on the cheek was all that was needed.

But when he arrived at the theater, Bronwyn was nowhere to be found. Kate assisted Miss Carew and

Gavin with their lines, and he sat on one of the benches to wait. He was pleased and a little surprised to hear Miss Carew's breathy interactions with the character who was meant to be her father had improved. She held herself at a discreet distance from his cousin, and Ben thought they might just convince their audience of her innocent, daughterly role opposite Gavin's Leonato.

Kate glanced up and smiled at him, and of course, that sent his thoughts spinning back to their luncheon the previous day. Despite his simple reply to Matthew, it had been more than fine. If not for Merryn's untimely arrival, they might very well have shared a *confection*.

He leaned forward, elbows on his knees, and studied his hands.

That he'd told Kate of Wilkins' invitation was no small matter. *No one* knew of the paper that burned a hole in his coat pocket. He still wasn't sure why he'd told her, but like a man testing a sore tooth, he'd *wanted* to see Kate's reaction. To hear her amused laughter and know he was, indeed, touched in the head for considering such a course.

But she'd not laughed. Instead, she'd been delighted that he should have such an opportunity. And if that weren't enough, she'd hidden the letter from his cousin. They'd been united in their shared secret, he and Kate. Something had shifted between them, and he felt... optimistic. Hope stirred in his chest, elusive and untetherable.

Miss Carew and his cousin finally moved off the stage, and Ben stood as Kate approached. He watched her for any indication she'd given their luncheon as much thought as he had, but her expression remained serene and composed. It betrayed nothing. Certainly, no hint that their lips had nearly touched, unless... Yes, there was a faint bit of color about her cheeks. Or perhaps the theater had simply grown overwarm.

He cleared his throat. "Have you seen Bronwyn?"

Kate's brows lifted a fraction at his lack of a proper greeting, but she said, "I have. She's gone to assist Morwenna with the costumes. I'm to stand in her stead."

Ben's breath caught in his throat. "You—you're to stand in for Bronwyn?"

"Yes."

"You're to stand in as Beatrice?" he clarified.

"Why, yes, of course."

"And we're to practice the final scene today?"

She gave him a brow-furrowed nod, and he couldn't blame her. He was behaving like a simpleton, but he couldn't stop himself from asking, "Have you read the final scene?"

She lifted her copy. "I was just about to do so."

She hadn't read the scene. She didn't know. Or did she? He couldn't remember all of his tutor's lessons, of course, but Kate had probably attended her governess's instruction with diligence. Did she recall Benedick and Beatrice's kiss?

At his frown, she said, "If you're in a rush, I can read as we go."

He released his frown and took a slow breath. "There's no rush, but... per'aps a little preparation ahead of the scene won't hurt."

"Um... all right. Why don't you have a seat while I review it?"

He waited on the bench, elbows back on his knees, while she read the scene. He watched as she turned the pages. When she neared the end, her eyes widened slightly. She licked her lips and he nearly groaned aloud.

"There's—there's a kiss in this scene," she said.

"Is there?"

The look she tossed him said he needed to work on his acting skills. "There is."

"'Tis a dilemma, to be sure. What do you suggest?"

She was silent for a long moment, and his heart nearly came to a stop. "Well... it *is* just for practice, and it's not as if I'll be the one playing the part of Beatrice in the actual performance. I suppose we could simply omit the kiss."

"Omit it?" Did he imagine her disappointment? He certainly didn't imagine his own, as he felt sure his heart shriveled just a bit.

Kate stared at his neckcloth, her brow creased in thought. "Or perhaps we could make do with a light peck on the cheek...?"

Make do? Beatrice and Benedick's love wasn't sealed with a *light peck*. His dismay must have shown for she watched him in silence for a moment. Finally, she smiled and her blush deepened.

"Mr. Kimbrell"—she only called him that in company or when she meant to tweak his dignity— "is this your way of stealing a kiss?"

His breath stopped for one... no, two heartbeats. He wasn't sure. When it resumed, he recalled all the pithy lines he'd imagined since their bonfire at Copper Cove. He swiftly reviewed and discarded each one, searching for an ace among so many deuces.

Finally, he gave her one word, his voice clear but soft. "Aye."

CHAPTER NINETEEN

B EN MEANT TO have his kiss. He waited, one
dark brow slightly higher than the other. They
stood close enough that she caught faint traces
of his shaving soap—that masculine, salty-sweet
scent that smelled of heather and the sea and Ben.

Miss Carew and Gavin had gone, the marriage-
minded ladies not yet arrived. The theater was
quiet, save the sound of Kate's own pulse. Ben's
manner held all the careless arrogance she expected,
but there was something else… something a bit
more intense about his gaze as it caressed her face.
There was a weight to it that wasn't normally there.

It was only a kiss, she told herself. Nothing more
than a gentle touch of Ben's lips to hers. It would be
fleeting, really—ended before it was even begun.

Except it wasn't *only* a kiss. It would never be
so with Ben.

He watched her, waiting, giving her a choice. She could respond with a teasing reply and let that be an end to it, or she could move them forward, past this dip in the road they'd never gotten their wheels through. She pulled in a breath for courage.

"Your cousin did say I'm not to allow you to leave out any important bits." Then she added for clarity, "I wish to do the scene as it's intended. With a kiss."

After a hesitation that seemed a lifetime, he nodded. "Bronwyn wants to ensure we deliver a proper performance."

"We wouldn't want to be seen as provincial."

With a barely-there smile, he extended his hand, and she allowed him to lead them to their places on the stage. Before they could begin, though, Ben lowered his copy and said, "Per'aps we ought to set the scene a bit."

He was right, of course. It had been some time since she'd read the play in its entirety, so a little scene setting would not go amiss. "Yes, of course."

"This is the final scene," he began, "where Benedick and Beatrice finally confess their love for one another. Leonato and Claudio are also present— I suppose I can read Gavin and Cadan's parts. The setting is Leonato's villa, where Hero and Claudio have just wed."

"It would be festive," she said, "but the balcony provides a welcome escape."

"Just so. Imagine the gardens below with trees and flowers—roses, perhaps, and some of those yellow blooms that grow outside your gate."

"Wild primrose."

He nodded. "Primrose then. The warmth of the day has released their fragrance to perfume the air. Climbing vines embrace the walls of the villa and spill onto the balcony while a carpet of bluebells dances in the distance."

"It sounds lovely," Kate said as she imagined the scene he described. She could smell the lush, damp soil of the garden and hear the trickling melody of a nearby fountain.

"Beatrice is veiled before she reveals herself to Benedick."

"Veiled. Of course." Kate's lips were dry with nerves and anticipation. She licked them and mentally urged Ben to hurry along with his scene setting.

"Our characters feel nervousness and anticipation for their encounter"—Kate darted a glance at him through her lashes—"but above all, they hold a deep and abiding affection for one another. Their words are teasing before their dialogue gradually becomes a sincere confession of their love. When we reach the final, culminating point where Benedick says, 'Peace! I will stop your mouth'—"

"Ben," Kate said somewhat urgently. "Why don't we just begin the scene?"

After a small hesitation, he nodded. "Of course." His smile, which was normally so certain, seemed a little unsteady. To her amazement, she realized he must be nervous too. It wasn't every day one kissed one's best friend, even for a play.

Ben's smile fell away altogether as they began reading, and his voice, which was always pleasing and deep, vibrated within her chest.

BENEDICK (to Beatrice): Do not you love me?

BEATRICE (after some hesitation): Why no, no more than reason.

BENEDICK: Why then, your uncle and the Prince and Claudio have been deceived. They swore you did.

BEATRICE: Do not you love me?

BENEDICK: Troth, no. No more than reason.

BEATRICE: Why then, my cousin, Margaret, and Ursula are much deceived, for they did swear you did.

BENEDICK: They swore that you were almost sick for me.

BEATRICE: They swore that you were well-nigh dead for me.

With each line spoken, the fluttering in Kate's chest increased its pace. Her fingers fiddled nervously with one another, and she forced her hands to still. And throughout the scene, Ben's voice remained firm and steady, anchoring her in this time and place. Her fingers relaxed and the pressure in her chest eased as she whispered, "I would not deny you, but by this good day, I yield upon great persuasion."

She waited in breathless anticipation for Ben to deliver his final line. His eyes, so dark a blue as to be almost black, found hers, and she thought she might drown in them. His upper lip was shadowed with the barest hint of whiskers above, and she imagined the pressure of his mouth against hers. He lifted one hand to her waist and the other to trace his thumb gently along the top of her cheek. His palm was smooth and rough at once, the weight of it warm against her skin. She leaned into him, her hands pressing the solid weight of his chest as he said softly, "Peace, I will stop your mouth." With the merest tensing of his jaw, he leaned close, and she closed her eyes—

"Mr. Kimbrell!"

Kate jumped, her eyes flying open as Mrs. Pentreath's cane thumped the theater's wooden floor. Leonato's gardens vanished with astonishing speed to leave her standing on the bare stage, Ben mere inches from her. Dazed, she stepped out of his arms and instantly felt the loss of his warmth.

Mrs. Pentreath sailed toward them, a trail of matrons fanning in her wake like ducklings.

"Were they kissing?" someone whispered.

Mrs. Pentreath came to a stop before the stage. "What is the meaning of this?" She punctuated the question with her cane. Before either of them could collect their wits, the lady's gaze spun to Kate. "Miss Parker, I expected better of you. To be sure, your father will be disappointed when he learns of this… this impropriety, to say nothing of Lady Catherine."

Kate closed her mouth, which had remained open during Mrs. Pentreath's march. Her attention went helplessly to the other matrons, who were nodding and shaking their heads in varying degrees of agreement and dismay. Behind them, Miss Brightbury's contingent crowded the theater entrance, craning their necks to see what drama had preceded their arrival.

"Well," Mrs. Pentreath said, "what have you to say for yourself, Mr. Kimbrell? Such an indiscretion cannot go unanswered."

Mrs. Clifton pushed her way forward to stand beside Mrs. Pentreath. "Does this mean we're finally to have an announcement from the pair of you?"

"What nonsense, Agnes," Mrs. Pentreath said. "There's nothing else for it."

"But Mrs. Pentreath," Kate began.

Before she could continue, though, Mrs. Tretheway emerged. "There's no telling how long the impropriety has persisted, and under our very noses. I saw them walking together on the lane above the Simmons cottage. Alone."

"I saw them as well."

"I heard there was an embrace."

Kate's head spun at the volley of accusations. "But that was one outing," she said.

"Do you think Eve argued she'd only had the one bite?"

"One discretion may as well be fifty."

A wedge of light opened behind them, and Bronwyn rushed into the theater, followed closely by Wynne and Morwenna. She stopped short to see the crowd gathered before the stage. Kate narrowed her eyes as she realized the trick her friend had played. Mrs. Pentreath would never have countenanced kissing in their performance, and she was certain Bronwyn knew it. That Kate should have known it—that she'd willfully ignored such logic—was beside the point.

Ben's jaw was tight as he looked out at their audience. "Enough," he said. The word was low but spoken with authority, and the theater quieted. Ben lifted Kate's hand. The gentle pressure of his fingers drew her eye to his, and she found refuge in his gaze. Her heart, which had skipped so painfully just moments before, found its rhythm, and she curled her fingers into his palm.

His gaze remained on hers as he spoke to Mrs. Pentreath. "You may be the first to congratulate us, ma'am. Miss Parker and I are to marry."

———

MISS PARKER AND I are to marry. The words hung in the air, resonating like the parish church bell. Certainly, there'd never been a statement as simple as it was complex. Kate's hand was soft in his, but she tensed with uncertainty at his words.

Wynne and Morwenna looked slightly aghast at his announcement while Bronwyn clasped her hands before her in... pleasure? Satisfaction? A prayer for deliverance?

Ben scowled and dismissed the lot of them. "If you all will excuse us, my *betrothed* and I need a word."

Mrs. P eyed him with suspicion, but she remained silent as he led Kate off the stage. They found a quiet corner away from the matrons' prying eyes and not-so-quiet whispers. He dropped Kate's hand, which had gone cold, and took two steps back to allow her room to breathe.

The air in the theater had grown heavier somehow, and he was having difficulty himself. He rubbed a hand along his forehead and forced a slow breath into his lungs. He couldn't say he was disappointed, precisely, with the day's events, but what of Kate? She couldn't like having her future chosen for her in such a manner.

"Marriage?" she said in a low whisper, and her disbelieving tone confirmed his thoughts. "Surely, there's no need for anything so... so drastic."

Ben swallowed and looked over her head. Mrs. P wore a self-satisfied expression as she gathered her flock about her. The news of Ben and Kate's indiscretion—not to mention their resulting betrothal—would spread within minutes.

"Kate," he said gently, "they saw us in an embrace. They would have seen more had they arrived but a moment later."

Her cheeks pinkened in the shadows. "But marriage?" she repeated. "We've never even shared a kiss." Her eyes turned down the merest bit at the corners, and he took courage in her disappointment.

"I think 'tis best if I speak with your father as soon as possible."

"My father? Oh! Yes, of course. I suppose you're right." Her expression, which had been clouded with shock, cleared. "I wouldn't want him to hear of this from anyone else." She closed her eyes and swallowed as something else occurred to her. "Or my grandmother."

The door opened and Mrs. P and the matrons made their way from the theater, no doubt to begin spreading the tale. Ben's jaw tightened.

"Bronwyn is here," he said. "Will you be all right if I leave you with her?"

Her gaze narrowed at the mention of his cousin, and he was pleased to see the light return to her eyes. He thought he could divine her thoughts. He had a few of his own in Bronwyn's direction, as he felt certain he and Kate had been *managed*. Not that they hadn't been willing participants in Bronwyn's scheme, but that was rather beside the point.

"Yes," she said and her voice firmed. "She and I have a few matters to discuss."

He lifted her hand in his once more and dropped a kiss onto the back of her knuckles. Her fingers trembled slightly in his, and he squeezed her gently before releasing her hand. "Leave something of my cousin for the undertaker," he whispered. He was pleased to have startled a laugh from her.

CHAPTER TWENTY

KATE SLIPPED THROUGH the theater's back entrance to make her way home in solitude. Although she'd told Ben she wished to speak with Bronwyn, she needed to collect her wits first.

He'd gone some moments before and, on his horse, would soon be rounding the final curve near her home. He would meet with her father soon. She paused on the path and closed her eyes to let the full weight of *that* sink in. There was no turning back from this. Ben was right—there'd been no recourse for them once Mrs. Pentreath and the matrons arrived. She and Ben would marry. A swarm of bees spiraled in her stomach, equal measures of anticipation and anxiety.

It was true the tenor of their friendship had changed over the past weeks. It had grown deeper and richer, and though neither of them had spoken of a future together, she'd begun to think what-ifs. Given time, she thought—hoped—they might have found their way to something more than friendship, but now they were being marched along at a rapid clip. It was all too soon.

Ben had only just begun to reveal his innermost thoughts and desires—sharing Mr. Wilkins' letter had been a revelatory start—but much of his heart remained firmly locked away. What was he thinking now? Did he worry over what marriage would mean for his opportunities in London? He must, for how could he afford to take on a wife *and* a new post with Mr. Wilkins? The bees swooped and dove, and she pressed a hand against her stomach to soothe the unease there.

She wasn't to have her solitude for long, as footfalls soon crunched the path behind her. She turned to see Bronwyn walking with hurried steps, her skirts lifted a trifle too high for propriety.

Her friend reached her, gasping, and Kate dispensed with a greeting. "What were you thinking, to give me a *kissing* scene to practice with Ben?" Even as she said the words, guilt stained her cheeks. Bronwyn may have given her the instrument for the day's disaster, but Kate had chosen to play it. That knowledge didn't ease her irritation, though.

Bronwyn clutched one hand to her chest and

pulled in a few deep breaths. Kate waited impatiently, arms crossed, until Bronwyn finally said, "Are you very angry with me then? You have every right to be. I have meddled in the worst way, but 'tis only because I love the pair of you so."

Kate spun and continued walking, taking perverse pleasure in Bronwyn's shortened breath as she hurried to keep pace.

"Well," Bronwyn said on an exhale, "was it nice at least? The kiss, that is. I don't need details, o' course. Please don't give me details, but at least tell me if—"

"There was no kiss."

"What?" Bronwyn stopped and Kate was forced to stop with her or speak over her shoulder.

"There was no kiss," she repeated. "Mrs. Pentreath arrived too s—that is, Mrs. Pentreath arrived."

"Well, then… why on earth must you marry? Not that I don't think 'tis a splendid idea, but if there was no kiss…"

"There was almost a kiss," Kate clarified.

"Almost a kiss? What d'you mean? Never say my cousin missed *again*?"

With an unladylike snort, Kate turned and continued up the lane. She was *not* explaining this to Bronwyn. She could still feel the gentle press of Ben's hand about her waist, the warm stroke of his thumb along her cheekbone. The solid weight of his chest beneath her hands. The bees swarmed again, though not unpleasantly, and Kate bit her lip.

Bronwyn fell into step beside her and they walked in silence for several paces, each lost in their own thoughts. Finally, with a bone-deep sigh, Bronwyn said, "Kate, 'tis time for some plain speaking."

Kate sent her a sideways glance. "Regarding?"

"As much as I would love to have you for a sister, you and my brother simply don't suit. There. I've said it."

"Merryn?" Kate pulled her head back at the unexpected turn in the conversation. It occurred to her then that, although she'd abandoned her aims where Bronwyn's brother was concerned, she'd not said as much to Bronwyn.

"Surely, you must see it," Bronwyn continued. "I know he's respectable and dependable and all that rot, but I would suggest his greatest appeal for you is that he *doesn't* return your affections."

Kate frowned. "Bronwyn..."

"I know," Bronwyn said, holding a hand, palm out, against Kate's unspoken protest. "'Tis a bold statement, but it makes an odd sort of sense. Nurturing an interest in my brother allowed your heart to remain happily unengaged—"

"Bronwyn."

"—while you satisfied your notion of what a young, marriageable lady is supposed to do with her time."

"What we're supposed to do with our time?" Kate started walking once more, and Bronwyn looped an arm through hers.

"Precisely. We're meant to be interested in courting and marriage and making a family with an eligible gentleman. My brother fits the bill rather nicely, without the annoyance of actually having to proceed with any of't."

When Bronwyn paused to draw breath, Kate said, "I've no interest in your brother."

"'Tis easy enough to see your heart's already taken. The sooner you know it too, the—wait. What?"

Kate studied a loose thread on her sleeve, but she couldn't help the smile that threatened her lips. "I'm not interested in forming a match with Merryn. Nor, I suspect, is he. My heart is already taken."

It was true. It had been for some time, ever since that first spring in Cornwall. And now, she would make a life with Ben. Bear his children. Spend the rest of her days with him. Kiss him, and more. Though they'd been denied the experience, she knew kissing Ben would be a pleasant diversion. Invigorating, even, judging by the swift dip of her stomach whenever she allowed herself to indulge her imagination.

Bronwyn, seeing her expression, squealed. "I knew it! Only imagine, you'll be a married lady soon enough. You can enjoy all the kisses you like," she said, pressing Kate's arm. "Aaaand you can tell your maiden friends all the best bits. Well, some of them, per'aps. To be sure, I don't need to hear *every*thing...."

Bronwyn continued talking, and Kate only hoped she and Ben didn't come to regret their path. As much as she might enjoy a lifetime of kisses with Ben, she didn't think she could bear it if she never had his heart.

———

THE QUIET THAT met Kate when she entered her home's marble-floored hall was absolute. She supposed it must have been her thoughts lending their weight to the air, but even Henderson's genial face was more staid than usual as he took her gloves and bonnet.

"Henderson, where is my grandmother?"

"Lady Catherine is in the front parlor with Miss Alys."

"And my father?"

"In the library with Mr. Kimbrell." Henderson's gaze didn't betray even a hint of what he was thinking.

Kate smoothed her skirts and, with a steadying breath, strode toward the parlor.

"Kate," Alys said in an excited whisper when she entered. "Ben is in the library with Papa. He seems exceedingly serious. Do you think someone has died?"

Kate swallowed. Was that how he saw their betrothal—as a death? But no, that was only Alys's fanciful imagination.

Her sister, undeterred by Kate's silence, continued chattering about Ben's curious demeanor. Their grandmother ruffled a bejeweled hand through her terrier's white fur, but on seeing Kate's expression, she stilled. With rank and authority lacing her tone, she said, "Alys, allow me a moment with your sister."

Alys stopped mid-sentence, and a line formed between her brows as she looked between the two of them. "Something has happened," she said slowly. "What has happened?"

"Alys," Kate warned softly.

Her sister rose with surprising grace and carried herself from the room. Only the barest sniff of irritation was heard as she went.

"Your sister will be her own undoing," Lady Catherine said.

Kate nodded, lips flattened in a wry expression. "You realize she merely waits beyond the door?"

"Alys," Lady Catherine said in a tone that brooked no argument. She'd not raised her voice, but it had carried, nonetheless. Even sound, it seemed, fell to her grandmother's will.

A muffled "drat" was heard through the wood, followed by a considering pause and finally the click of her sister's footsteps on the marble.

Kate sat on the striped silk settee and arranged her skirts over her knees. "Grandmother," she began, resisting the urge to chew her lip. She then related (some of) what had occurred at the theater. Of course, she left out the more descriptive bits leading up to the matrons' arrival, but she ended with, "And now, Ben and I—we're to be married. If Papa approves, that is."

Kate waited, hands folded, as her grandmother's assessing eye studied her. Finally, Lady Catherine said, "I surmised as much from Mr. Kimbrell's audience with your father. I can't say the Circumstances are ideal, but a lady of your years can't be Too Particular. I only wish you'd consulted me first."

"Grandmother?"

"It's unfortunate we couldn't have contrived A Situation with the cousin instead." Silence fell as her grandmother's words hung between them.

"Did you say—do you think I planned for this to happen?" Kate asked softly.

Lady Catherine released her dog to give Kate's hand a gentle pat. It was the most physical interaction she'd had from her grandmother since... well, ever. "A lady does what she must."

There was no time to respond to that as the parlor doors swung open. Her father entered, followed by Ben.

"Katie?" Her father's gaze, normally one of inattentive distraction, was sharp as he studied her, and concern lined the corners of his eyes.

She answered his unspoken question with a nod. "All is well, Papa."

Her eyes went next to Ben, and she was struck by how much older he appeared—more mature, even—than when he'd returned from London only a few short weeks before. Though there was a tightness about his eyes, his posture was composed as his gaze sought hers.

Her grandmother stood and passed the dog to Henderson, who held the squirming canine from his immaculate suit. Kate barely noticed when they all quit the room, so loud was the thumping of her heart.

Ben crossed the parlor to take the seat next to her, his steps silent on the thick carpet. His voice was steady as he said, "'Tis done."

Kate's brows lifted. Two words, and she was an engaged lady. How much different was her life now than just an hour before? She nodded and pressed the muslin of her skirts over her knees once more. He stilled her hands with one of his own, the pressure of his fingers against her skin warm and pleasing as his thumb stroked the back of her hand.

"Will you tell me what you're thinking?" she asked.

After a too-long pause, he said, "I'm thinking we are friends, you and I. I imagine we'll go along nicely as husband and wife."

"Yes," she agreed, pleased with how her voice didn't quaver.

His gaze searched hers. Then, with a shallow nod, he rose and left the room.

CHAPTER TWENTY-ONE

TO KATE'S SURPRISE, life as an engaged lady was little changed. She assisted Morwenna and Bronwyn with the final trims to the costumes, with nary a sleeve stitched to her own skirts, while Ben continued his work on the sets. She gathered that he rose before the sun and burned the candles to stubs during the night. They'd seen little of one another over the past week.

To her untrained eye, there was still a good bit of work required on the sets. They must be painted and installed on the rotating platform Ben had designed. Plants and pots must be gathered to form the villa's garden, and all must be arranged in time for the final rehearsals.

It was to that end that Kate donned her oldest gown and an apron and awaited Ben's arrival at her father's glasshouse. By the time he entered, looking too handsome by half with his hair blown about by the wind, she'd set aside a number of old pots.

"Good afternoon," he said, walking toward her with long strides. As he neared, she could see the lines about his eyes. He didn't look like a newly-engaged gentleman on the brink of everlasting happiness. He appeared a bit... worn about the edges.

He glanced down and an expression of surprise crossed his face. "You're wearing the gloves."

She turned her hands to show him she was, indeed, wearing his gift. "They're lovely, don't you think?"

"You make them so," he said, and her stomach dipped alarmingly. "But," he added with a throat-clearing, "you don't need them."

"I thought we were preparing the plants today."

"We are." And, then reaching for her hand, he slid one of the buttons from its loop.

"But I—" She stopped, mesmerized by his fingers as he managed another button and another before gently tugging the leather from her fingers.

"Don't you wish to feel the dirt?"

His grin was slow as was her answering smile. He jerked his chin to indicate the pot at her side. She flexed her fingers before dipping them into the damp soil. Oh, it was glorious!

"I think you will make the most wonderful of

husbands," she said, though the words felt a bit foreign on her tongue. He must have thought so as well because the lines about his eyes tightened a bit.

They spoke of little of consequence while they worked, and her hands were well and delightfully ruined by the time Ben loaded the last of the pots onto his father's cart.

"Shall I come help you arrange them?" she offered.

"Tomorrow, per'aps. I've a bit more to finish on the villa's interior, and the platform mechanism catches, so there's a bit of refining still to be done. All that remains after that is to paint the backdrops and install our balcony, then we can see to arranging the garden."

Frowning, she watched him climb atop the seat. She removed her dirt-stained apron as he directed the horse toward the lane. His list of "all that remains" sounded like more than one man could reasonably accomplish. Time was running short before the play would open, but Ben remained determined to do it all himself.

She understood his need for perfection. She even admired his exacting standards. She gathered that he might have felt a need to prove himself, given Newford's frequent reminders of Kimbrell's Folly. But none of that meant he must bear the weight of their balcony alone.

The daylight was fading, but she rushed inside and washed her hands, scrubbing until the soil was gone from her nails. She collected her determination, then Bronwyn, and the pair set out to find Merryn.

His family's building firm was well situated near Newford's small harbor. Kate had never had occasion to visit him there, but Bronwyn assured her Merryn would be happy to receive them. They found him in his office, a small but tidy space with a large desk and an even larger worktable spread edge to edge with drawings. If he was surprised by their arrival, he hid it well and rose to greet them. After pleasantries were exchanged, Kate went straight to the reason for their visit.

"I've come to request that you send some of your men to assist with the sets tomorrow," she said. "And preferably someone who knows how to mix paints."

Merryn settled back in his chair—a great, leather tufted affair—and eyed the pair of them. "Has Ben sent you?"

Kate hesitated, fearing she might have overstepped. "He's unaware I've come."

Merryn's smile was gentle. "Miss Parker, you and I both know my cousin has only to say the word and he'll have the aid he needs."

She stared at him in bewilderment until it occurred to her. "You're waiting until he asks for help," she said slowly.

"I'm waiting 'til he's ready to accept help. There's a distinction."

Kate considered the polished surface of his desk before tossing his words back to him. "You and I both know that will be a long wait."

Merryn rubbed his jaw as he studied them. "You're probably correct in that," he finally said, "but 'tis a matter of pride, you understand."

Kate frowned at such an unhelpful answer, especially after their earnest conversation outside the Feather. She thought he might say more, but he remained silent. As she was trying to think of a polite way to tell him to stuff his pride, Bronwyn stood.

"Hang pride," her friend said with no little heat.

Merryn's lips twitched at his sister's words, and his gaze shifted back to Kate in question.

She nodded once. "Precisely."

"Very well." His shrug was not one to instill confidence.

———

THE NEXT DAY, Ben arrived early at the theater, surprised and a bit unnerved to find it already humming with activity. The sun was barely risen, but some dozen or more of his brothers and cousins made a merry bunch. They bustled about, their voices echoing in the empty space as they worked like so many brawny elves.

Over the past weeks, Ben had negotiated a collection of worn sails from Newford's fishermen and tasked Morwenna with patching them. They were a bit ragged about the edges, but once painted, the canvases would serve as picturesque backdrops until they were returned to their proper service. To be sure, Newford's luggers would be the envy (or the laughingstock) of the area's fishermen as they plied the coast with their newly-painted rigging.

But the sails, which had been neatly stacked along one wall, now hung from the rafters, thanks to his kin's industry. To find them unrolled when he'd not given the least bit of direction for their painting caused anxiety to crawl along Ben's neck. Thank the heavens he'd arrived before anyone had a chance to do more. He quickly found Alfie among the lot, mixing a pot of paint as if he had the least notion what, precisely, needed painting. With effort, Ben fixed a smile on his face and strode toward his brother.

"What are you doing?" he asked.

"And a good morning to you," Alfie said, tossing a grin over his shoulder. "Before you grumble your displeasure at me, you should know 'tis all your betrothed's doing. She's an uncommon amount of good sense."

Alfie motioned across the theater, and Ben turned to see Kate, crouched before her own pot of paint and stirring diligently. She was partially hidden by one of the hanging canvases, else his eyes surely would have found her first. She looked up and caught his gaze, and Ben thought she appeared a little uncertain. As well she should if she was, as Alfie said, the reason for the day's collective.

He turned to go to her, but Alfie stopped him with his next words. "You've done well in choosing Miss Parker," he said, standing and wiping his hands on a cloth. "'Tis a rare thing to marry a friend, and we're all that pleased you've finally found your wits."

"Thank you. I think."

Alfie leaned close to add in confidence, "If you find yourself in need of advice, I count myself skilled at navigating marital waters. They can be tricky if you don't know the way of the shoals and currents."

Ben snorted and, with clearly worded instructions not to touch a paintbrush to a single canvas, he turned his feet toward Kate.

She'd returned to her task, but she must have heard his approach for she set the pot aside and stood. She wore a charming bit of blue paint on one cheek, and he itched to wipe it away. To hold her soft cheek beneath his hand once more. They'd never finished their kiss, and the incompleteness of it was like a breath drawn but not released.

He lifted his hand to wipe his thumb gently across the paint. There were too many people about for more than that simple gesture, but his thumb, rather than clearing the paint away, dragged it across her cheek to leave a thin blue smear. He frowned and lowered his hand as she watched him in confusion.

"You had a bit of paint," he explained, turning his hand for her to see. Clearing his throat, he returned his attention to the activity around them. "What's all this?"

She licked her lips once before replying. "There's not much time left before the play opens. I thought we could use a bit of help to see the canvases painted."

"I don't—" Ben had come with a gentle reproach for Kate's interference, well-intentioned though it may have been, but her words stopped him. Or rather, one word. *We. We could use a bit of help.* His brows pinched together, not so much in displeasure but in thought. To be fair, he and Kate had taken on the task of the sets together. He wasn't the only one who stood to lose if they didn't succeed.

Over her shoulder, he watched as Alfie's wife joined his brother, the two of them putting their heads together over Alfie's paint pot. Alfie and Eliza were a pair. A matched set. And now, Ben and Kate were to be the same. His jaw flexed as he considered the incredible turn his life had taken.

"Before you become angry," Kate continued, "consider that your brothers and cousins haven't done anything but hang a few canvases and mix a bit of paint. I've asked them to await your direction before moving forward."

The tension in Ben's shoulders eased a tiny fraction as he looked about. It was true—his kin hadn't done any more than what she said.

"And if it's merely pride that causes your hesitation, then"—she paused as if gathering her courage—"then *hang* pride, I say."

Though she'd spoken the words softly, for his ears alone, she'd not accounted for the theater's surprisingly good acoustics. The air about them stilled as his cousins paused what they were doing. Kate must have felt it too, for the color rose in her cheeks.

A smile threatened Ben's lips, and a bit more of his tension eased as he gave in to his laughter. "'Hang pride'?" he said, wiping his eyes. "I fear you've been too much in Bronwyn's company."

"Perhaps. Although in this case, your cousin's words are appropriate." Kate's eyes narrowed on him, though he detected the merest twitch of her lips. She was doing her best to maintain her dignity, and he forced himself to sober.

"I'm not angry," he assured her. "But I wish the sets to be…" It had been on the edge of his tongue to say *perfect*, and she seemed to know it as her brows dipped above her nose. In that moment, with a bit of blue paint smeared across the top of one cheek, Kate was the most perfectly imperfect princess he'd ever seen. Oh, he knew the paint was insignificant, but the symbolism of it found purchase in his mind. The fear roiling in his stomach—for her, for them, for their marriage—eased and he could finally draw a breath. All would be well. Not easy or perfect, but well. And it would be enough.

"I wish the sets to be worthy," he finished.

She leaned close to whisper, "And they will be."

"Ben," Gavin called to him from across the stage. "'Tis true you'll be compensating our efforts with ale at the Feather?"

Ben lifted a brow at his betrothed, who said, "I thought it only fair to offer some recompense, and your cousins do seem rather fond of ale."

"Aye," Ben replied to the group at large. "But only for the worthiest of you."

CHAPTER TWENTY-TWO

B EN'S FAMILY HAD finally gone, and the theater was still once more. They'd made surprisingly short work of the canvases. Although his brothers' notion of a proper Italian tree differed from Ben's own, he was forced to admit that once he got himself over his initial unease, their assistance was not wholly unwelcome. That wasn't to say he hadn't been vocal in his instruction or that he hadn't pecked at them like an old hen, but as the hours wore on and the canvases came alive with the colors of an Italian countryside, his smile had come a bit easier.

The canvases would hang overnight to dry. Tomorrow, they'd be rolled and secured to the rafters until the scene required a sunny orchard or a church with a (somewhat crooked) tree. All that remained was to install the final pieces of the balcony and Leonato's villa before they could set the final props in place.

He retrieved his tools from behind the stage and set to work. He wasn't sure how much time had passed before he became aware of another presence in the theater. Lowering his hammer, he stood to find Merryn studying the hanging canvases.

"'Tis impressive," Merryn said without turning. "Although I might have drawn the tree at the church from a different angle."

Ben grimaced. "Aye. 'Twould seem my brothers have provided their own perspective."

Merryn snorted at that then stepped onto the stage with Ben. "You've nearly finished installing the balcony?"

"'Twill be ready in time for the final rehearsals."

Merryn's gaze caught Ben's as he said, "'Tis a fine bit of work you've done, but nothing less than I expected."

Ben opened his mouth to remind his cousin of the tree, and to point out a rough place on one of the balustrades that required more sanding. The rotating dais caught as it turned and would require a bit more adjustment before Ben was satisfied. But he drew a long breath and released it before saying, "Thank you."

Merryn appeared as surprised as Ben by his accepting the compliment. Ben thought he might offer further comment, but his cousin merely cleared his throat and reached for another hammer. Ben only hesitated a moment before returning his own hammer to the task.

They worked for a time without speaking, the sound of their tools echoing in the empty theater. Finally, because it needed to be addressed, Ben said, "You've heard I'm betrothed?"

"Aye," Merryn said around a mouthful of nails. He sat back on his heels and removed them to add, "And a finer match you'll never find than Miss Parker. You've my congratulations, though I question the lady's wisdom."

Ben snorted a soft laugh. "You've the right of it." He hesitated before adding, "You're not disappointed that she's to wed another?"

"I couldn't be more pleased that she's to wed *you*. 'Tis as it should be."

Ben lowered his hammer and straightened, more relieved at his cousin's words than he cared to admit. Though he'd never believed Merryn's heart had truly been set on Kate, a tiny part of him had worried over the matter. They were cousins, after all.

Merryn had once been as close to him as one of his own brothers, in fact, but ever since the death of Ben's uncle, conversations between them had been like this one—brief and stilted with so much left unsaid. He'd grown weary of the weight that seemed to pull at his soul, choking and suffocating.

If he meant to begin a life with Kate, he wished to do so with a lighter heart.

"I'm sorry." The words were barely audible, so he added more firmly, "For what happened with your father." It had been more than a decade since his uncle's death. How was it possible he'd never spoken the words before?

Merryn paused, hammer suspended. He slowly brought his arm down, but he didn't look up. Ben sat, leaning against the back wall of the stage, one knee bent. He scrubbed a hand over his face, and when he opened his eyes, Merryn was lowering himself next to him.

"You've nothing for which to apologize," Merryn said slowly. "'Twas a long time agone, and you weren't to blame for what happened."

"I tried to help him, but—" Ben stopped and blinked at the moisture that burned his eyes. He cleared his throat and began again. "You weren't there that day, but he never would have fallen if I hadn't left my tools about." He inhaled once and blew the breath out again slowly. There. He'd said it. He'd always wondered if Merryn knew—if someone had told him or his mother of Ben's carelessness. The truth had been wrapped so tightly within him that it had grown impossibly heavy. Now that it was out, something inside him loosened, despite the shame of his admission.

Merryn tucked his chin before saying, "'Tis that what you think—that you were at fault for what happened? My father never would have fallen if he'd tied his rope. You remember he was always a stickler about us tying our ropes, but when it mattered, he didn't tie his own."

Ben cut a sharp look at his cousin. "*You're* a stickler about the rope."

Merryn's gaze was one of confusion. "And where d'you think I came by the notion?"

"I thought 'twas because of what happened with your father."

"Aye, but he'd required the habit in me—in us— well before that. D'you not remember your first time on the slates?"

Ben stared at a knot in the stage floor as he searched his memory. It had been years since he'd stood on rooftops with his uncle, but an image slowly formed of one particular morning. It had been brisk, the fog coming off the sea to blanket the coast as it often did. Ben and Merryn had stood near the edge of a low rooftop and peered at Newford below them, tucked in its wool wadding.

Ben thought they must have been atop Mr. Clifton's bakery with the Feather across the way, but it felt as though he'd reached the top of the world. It had been his first time to be so high, and he'd been proud to finally be taken up with his uncle and older cousin. Pedrek's calloused hands looped coils of coarse rope as he spoke in his firm but gentle tone.

"Listen well, lad, and heed the ropes. They may be your saving one day. Now, Merryn, ye've done this afore. Show young Benedick the way. Tie one end about yerself and the other round the chimney stack. Make the knots fast."

Merryn did as his father instructed, brow furrowed in concentration as his fingers worked the thick rope.

"Now, Benedick, ye take the other rope and secure it as yer cousin did."

Ben fumbled with the rope, his young hands struggling to mimic his cousin's actions. As he worked, Merryn grumbled in the tone of one issuing a well-worn complaint, "Da, nobody else does this."

"Aye, but 'tis a treacherous trade we're in, lads, and yer life be worth more than yer pride. And," he added with a wink, "a man would be pure and daft not to be afeared o' your mothers." He gave a quick tug to check the security of Ben's rope and nodded. "Aye, lad, ye have it then."

Ben's breath came back in a rush as memories flickered in his mind in fits and flashes. His uncle's large hands and rough voice. The kindness in his eyes and the quirk of his smile, which Merryn now carried. Now that he'd allowed himself to recall the events of that singular afternoon, they were as vivid as if he'd lived them yesterday. How could he have forgotten his uncle's ropes?

But then, Pedrek's death had drawn a clear line on the map of his life, a bold mark separating before from after. Whole from broken. Action from inaction.

Merryn shifted on the hard stage boards next to him, watching and waiting. "He didn't tie his rope," Ben said slowly, still not quite believing it. But it must have been true, else his uncle wouldn't have fallen to his death.

"No."

"He was always going on about the rope, wasn't he?"

"He was."

Ben wasn't ready to loosen his grip on his guilt. He'd left his tools where they shouldn't have been, after all. But to know he'd not been wholly responsible for his uncle's death caused something to shift and slide a bit inside. His soul, perhaps. His very essence.

With the horror of that day so many years before and his guilt over what had happened, he'd built a sturdy defense, brick by brick. The tragedy of his uncle's death was no less today, but for the first time, he thought there might be a bit of light seeping around the bricks.

He searched his mind for more memories of his uncle, cautiously allowing them into his thoughts and turning each carefully. "Your father had a rare talent for jokes. D'you remember the one he told us about the turnscrew?"

Merryn chuckled. "I had forgotten that one, but aye." He pitched his voice into a gravelly imitation of his father. "The turnscrew asked the screw, 'What d'ye think of me?'"

"I must say, you've completely turned my head," Ben replied, bemused that such a poor joke had once sent them into fits. They laughed now at the ridiculousness of it, but when Merryn brushed a hand over his eyes, Ben sobered. "You've done a proper job with your father's business," he said softly. "To be sure, he would have been proud of what you've made of it."

"D'you think so?"

"Aye."

Merryn cleared his throat. "Now that you're to be married, will you be making more trips to London, d'you think?"

Ben rubbed a hand on his jaw, which had tightened along with his shoulders. He'd been waiting for just this question, wondering when Merryn would ask for more details about his latest travels or his plans for future visits to London. It was a subject he avoided whenever possible—and he made sure it was *always* possible—as he'd no wish to think on, much less discuss, his hopes for the future. Hopes which had never quite withstood the weight of his doubts.

His cousin's tone had been casual, as if Merryn had no more interest in Ben's response than if he'd asked his opinion on the weather. But Ben could tell by the set of Merryn's shoulders that he expected an evasive reply. And that was a wearying thought—that his own kin should have such a view of him. Had he grown so tedious? He rather thought he might have.

He forced his muscles to relax. Reaching into his coat, he removed his letter, passing it silently to Merryn. His cousin took the paper with a bemused expression, but at Ben's nod, he unfolded it. His brows notched higher as he read, but he carefully cleared all expression from his face before he looked up. Ben *had* grown tedious indeed if his family felt the need to guard themselves so carefully around him.

With a sigh for his idiocy, he took the paper from Merryn and refolded it. Without any prompting from his cousin, he offered, "I need to discuss the matter with Kate, of course, but if I take Wilkins up on his offer, you'll need to find another to do your slate work."

Merryn's lips twitched as he fought a smile, and Ben hid his frown as he tucked the letter back into his coat.

"I said 'if,' you bleddy fool," he grumbled.

CHAPTER TWENTY-THREE

BEN HONORED KATE'S bargain and joined his cousins at the Feather. They were a boisterous bunch as they enjoyed their compensation and a plate of Wynne's raspberry tarts. His betrothed had displayed exceedingly good sense in organizing the day's effort, else he'd still be burning the candles down.

His *betrothed*. The word still didn't sound real. It was like something from a dream, made up and imaginary and all the more so for being attached to Kate. How much odder would he feel when he called her *wife*? The word echoed in his mind as if he'd spoken it aloud, and he hid his smile behind his cup.

"Now that you're betokened," Gavin said, "I imagine you'll have fewer jaunts to London, unless you plan to take your new bride."

Ben returned his ale to the table and wiped his mouth. The reminder that the rest of his cousins—his own brothers, even—knew nothing of the reason for his travels to London brought an unwelcome tightness to his chest. His cousins had eagerly quizzed him on each of his journeys. They wouldn't be pleased to know he'd kept the true nature of his travels from them, but Ben owed them all the truth, and he was, oddly enough, ready to finally have it out.

"As to that," he began. When he finished explaining how he'd made the acquaintance of Wilkins, and how his travels to London had been for the express purpose of studying architecture, his relations stared at him with varying degrees of amusement. All but Alfie, who wore a faint crease between his brows.

Gavin held his palm out and nodded at their cousins. Slowly, the crowd around the table tossed coins to spin on the polished oak, and Gavin collected them before they could roll to the floor.

"You had a *wager*?" Ben asked.

"I knew something was afoot," Gavin said as he pocketed his earnings. "Your tales have always been about this building or that, never the amusements to be had. To be sure, Cousin, if I ever travel to London, I'll find more entertaining ways to spend my time."

Ben snorted a soft laugh at this as his cousins debated what they would do if ever they found themselves in London. When Alfie rose from the table, Ben waited half a beat before following him. His brother dodged Peggy and a tray laden with ales to exit through the Feather's narrow door.

By the time Ben found him, Alfie lounged against the side of the inn, arms crossed as though waiting for him. The pair of them were closer in age than temperament, with only a couple of years separating them. But where Ben had always felt the weight of the past behind his smile, Alfie had a rare talent for finding happiness in all things. Even their mother's death hadn't brought him low, a fact which had angered Ben at the time. He'd never told his brother as much, though he suspected many of their youthful arguments had had their roots in Ben's anger.

Now, he leaned himself against the inn next to his brother. "You don't seem surprised."

A long moment passed before Alfie said, "That you've a talent for architecture? No. I'm that pleased to see you doing something about it. That you've been studying in London without telling anyone? Aye, I have to say 'twas a little unexpected, though, like Gavin, I always thought there must be more to your travels than what you've had us believe."

"I'm sorry I didn't tell you."

"I'm sorry you didn't feel you could."

Ben swallowed. "'Twasn't intentional at first,

keeping London to myself. It just seemed to… happen. I didn't know if I had the talent for the work, and if not, it would have been another Kimbrell's Folly if… everyone knew."

"Your brothers are not 'everyone.'"

"Aye."

"Does our father know?"

Ben nodded. He'd not, in good conscience, been able to keep the matter from their father, though now he wondered that he'd kept it from the rest of his family for so long.

"And Grandfather?"

Ben nodded again, miserably. "I needed my portion."

"Who else?" Alfie asked, and Ben pinched the bridge of his nose.

"Merryn," he admitted. "But only because he secured my introduction to Wilkins."

"And Kate, I imagine."

"And Kate, but that is all."

They stood in silence for a few moments longer before Alfie said, "You've always held your own counsel. Kept your thoughts close and your heart closer. I worried for you when Mother passed and again when Uncle Pedrek died. You seemed to keep everything so tightly bound inside."

Ben couldn't argue with his brother's assessment, but neither could he let it pass without comment.

"And you never seemed to mourn them properly." As soon as the words were out, Ben regretted them.

"I mourned them," Alfie said softly. "But I chose to keep the good memories in my heart and let go the rest." Alfie's gaze caught his and held as he said, "Choose happiness, Brother."

And that, Ben realized, was the difference between Alfie's smile and his own. Ben's had been nothing more than a masquerade all these years, a carefully maintained fiction, while his brother's came from a place of true peace. Ben wanted to find that peace. He *needed* to find it if he were to make a fitting husband for Kate. Could it be as simple as Alfie made it seem? Could he simply… choose?

He swallowed against the lump that had risen in his throat. Rubbing a hand over his eyes, he nodded. Alfie pushed away from the inn and clasped him in a brotherly embrace. Ben couldn't recall the last time he'd held one of his brothers in anything other than a wrestling hold. He gripped him hard, clutching Alfie's coat in his fists.

Some moments passed before Ben finally released him, embarrassed. Alfie looked away as any gentleman ought to do when faced with another man's tears. Ben pulled a handkerchief from his pocket and blew his nose as his brother said, "What will you do about London? Will you take Wilkins up on his offer?"

"I'm undecided."

"What does your betrothed make of it? Would she enjoy living in London, d'you think?"

Ben was silent as he tucked the handkerchief away, and Alfie sighed. "Can I offer one more bit of advice?"

Ben chuckled, though the sound was a bit watery. "You're full of advice this night, but aye."

"Now that you're to be married," Alfie said, "you'll be required to talk more. I suggest you begin by asking your betrothed what she thinks of living in London."

Ben knew his brother was right. It was past time for a proper conversation with Kate, but he couldn't let Alfie's advice go without a taunt or two. "I suppose six months of marriage is sufficient to make an expert of you."

"And you have been married for how long?"

"'Tis a fair point."

CHAPTER TWENTY-FOUR

B EN LEFT ALFIE to their cousins and made quick time up the lane to Kate's home. The moon was high to light his way, but the hour was late. He wasn't surprised to find the house dark when he arrived. Not a candle burned in any of the front windows.

His horse danced beneath him as he considered the stone manor's dark facade. The house was asleep, but was Kate still awake? He knew her window. He'd often seen her watching from it as he'd built his folly, so he turned the horse's head in that direction.

He slowly picked his way to the back of the house, and more than once, Ben hoped the Parker servants weren't in the habit of arming themselves. They'd surely shoot him before learning he meant the household no harm.

He finally reached the rear of the manor, but the windows along the back were as dark as the front had been. He counted until he found Kate's room, smiling to know she slept just a few short feet away.

As he prepared to leave—there was nothing else for it now—a candle flared. He stopped, and Kate appeared. The candle lit her face, revealing her surprise at finding him beneath her window. Her hair was down, and he couldn't recall ever seeing it so before.

In one smooth motion, she opened the window and leaned out, her hair swinging in a dark braid about her shoulders. She was a sight in naught but a thin night rail and dressing gown, her throat pale and bare above a thin line of lace trimming. Marriage, he thought, would agree with him if it meant he could enjoy such a sight every night for the rest of his life.

"Ben?" she said in an overloud whisper. "What are you doing?"

It was a moment before he could gather his wits to respond. "I need to speak with you."

"Now?" Her brows dipped in confusion before she gasped. "You haven't gotten it into your head to elope, have you?"

He couldn't resist teasing her. "What if I have?"

Even from this distance, he could see the

movement of her throat as she swallowed. "Tonight?" The word was barely audible on the still night air, and Ben's chest tightened. Kate didn't seem as opposed to the idea as he might have expected. He swiftly calculated the distance to the border before his better sense caught up. Her father and grandmother would have his head for such an escapade, and there was no reason for it, really.

"Who's eloping? Ben, is that you?" They'd woken Alys. Her pale face appeared two windows from Kate's as she peered along the house at her sister. "You're eloping?" she squealed. Ben wondered, given the volume of her gleeful tone, how much longer they had before the rest of the house awoke.

"No!" Kate said in a softer, though no less emphatic, tone. She returned her gaze to Ben, but there was a question in her eyes.

"We are not eloping," he confirmed for Alys. To Kate, he said, "I will speak with you tomorrow. My apologies for waking you." There would be no further discussion of their future tonight. He turned the horse to go, but Kate called down to him.

"Good night," she whispered, her gaze steady on him.

"Good night." From the corner of his eye, he saw that Alys still watched them, but he didn't care. He touched his fingers to his mouth and blew a kiss to Kate. Her smile was broad as she ducked back into her room.

———

THE NEXT MORNING, Ben woke before the sun. It was too early to return to Kate's home. In truth, it wasn't more than a handful of hours since he'd left her window. He was anxious to see her, to speak with her about their future. But it wouldn't do to present himself before a reasonable hour, so he worked some more on the sets.

There was more to finish on the villa's interior, and he still had the rough spot in the dais's rotating mechanism to address. When even that effort failed to settle his restlessness, he paced, and when that only agitated him further, he left the theater.

The thought that he might search out Merryn or one of his brothers to assist with the day's tasks occurred to him, though the notion still felt as foreign as a fish on land. He didn't know if he'd ever become accustomed to accepting, much less requesting, aid from others. But instead of waking one of his relations, he soon found himself on the lane to Simmons' cottage, of all places.

He didn't know why he went. Perhaps he only wished to assure himself he could choose a different future for himself than the one Simmons painted.

The morning mist hadn't yet lifted from the valley's low spots, and Simmons' home lay at the lowest part of the valley. Ben could barely pick out the wooden post at the end of the man's drive, but Nell's furious barking told him he'd arrived. The cottage was in the same sorry state as before, overgrown with weeds and despair, dark gaps spotting the roof where slates were missing. The chimney appeared cold again, without even a wisp of smoke to suggest anyone lived inside.

Ben walked carefully up the path, making certain not to stray too close to the end of the dog's tether, until he reached the safety of Simmons' porch. Given the man's fondness for drink, he didn't expect him to be risen, but he rapped firmly on the wood, nonetheless.

There was, predictably, no response, and he was about to leave when he heard the distinctive crack of an axe splitting wood from behind the house. Frowning, he skirted Nell's space to make his way around the edge of the cottage. Simmons' lanky frame stood before a low stump, a heavy axe suspended high above his head. With barely a glance for Ben, he swung, bringing the blade down to split the log cleanly.

"Kimbrell," Simmons said gruffly as he placed another log on the stump. He was taller than he'd been before, if such a thing were possible. His shirt, though wrinkled, appeared clean beneath his vest, and a dark felt hat shadowed his brow.

"Simmons." Ben returned the greeting with bemusement, disbelieving the man before him was the same one who'd stumbled from the theater only weeks before.

"'Tis true ye're finally to marry the Parker lass?"

"Aye."

Simmons nodded as he lifted the axe once more. "'Twill be good for ye, having a woman like that to warm your home." *Crack!* The log cleaved in two and Simmons placed another on the stump.

"To be sure, I don't deserve her." Ben was uncertain of many things, but that wasn't one of them.

"None of us deserve the ladies we're blessed with." Then, after a pause, Simmons asked, "Did ye finish yer theater business?"

"I've a few tasks still to do." Ben had been unsure why he'd made the walk to Simmons' home. He'd thought it had more to do with his own future than Simmons' but now he said, "Are your mind and senses clear?"

The older man's eyes narrowed, and Ben thought he might ignore the question to return to his log splitting. Finally, Simmons removed his hat and wiped his brow with the back of one forearm. "For the moment."

"I could use a carpenter. I've heard you're one of the best."

"'Tis true," Simmons said without conceit.

Ben jerked a thumb back toward Newford. "Come see what you can make of it then, but time is short."

Simmons gave him a single, short nod before setting his axe aside.

Ben kicked at a stray bit of broken slate as they walked. With a nod toward Simmons' roof, he said, "When we've finished, I'll help you patch the corner."

Simmons opened his mouth—on an argument, no doubt—then closed it again with an audible grinding of his teeth. Jerking his head in another single nod, he followed Ben to the lane.

They spent the next hours finishing sets. Ben showed Simmons the balcony he'd crafted, with its ornate balustrade and finely turned handrail, to which the old man grunted. Ben took it as an approval of sorts. But when he demonstrated the catch in the villa's rotating mechanism, Simmons unfolded his arms to rub at his jaw in curious speculation.

"The dais must turn without any impediment," Ben said. Simmons bent to inspect the under workings, the creak of his bones loud in the empty theater. When he stood, Ben handed him a sanding block, which Simmons took without comment. They worked in silence, sanding and oiling joints, until the dais turned easily.

By the time Ben made his way to Kate's home again, Henderson regretted to inform him she'd just left to visit an ailing neighbor.

———

THE SUN WAS beginning its slow descent toward the valley's edge by the time Kate returned home. She removed her gloves and bonnet and gave them into Henderson's waiting hands. "You've had a visitor, Miss Parker. Mr. Kimbrell came an hour past."

Ben? Her heart kicked against her ribs. Their midnight meeting had played in her mind long after he'd gone from beneath her window. In the tiny moment when she'd thought he meant for them to elope, her breath had caught. The romance of it had captured her imagination for a full minute before Ben confirmed the matter. *We are not eloping.* It had depressed her spirits nearly as much as his statement after the meeting with her father: *It is done.*

She'd been surprised by the disappointment that had flown through her on swift wings. Though she never would have credited it, she was no better than one of Alys's insensible heroines, to be so caught up by the notion of a midnight elopement.

But it was clear Ben had something he wished to discuss. Part of her worried he was having second thoughts about their marriage. The banns hadn't yet been called, but all of Newford knew of their betrothal. If he wished to back out of the thing now, it would be disastrous for both of them. But then she would recall the kiss he'd sent her from beneath her window. It hadn't been the careless sort of kiss one expected from a charming rogue. There'd been some weight to it. Promise and potential. And *that* had calmed her worries.

She'd risen early that morning and gone to the theater in search of him but had been surprised to find him absent. Now, she hurried toward the stairs. She'd repair her hair and change her gown then seek him out once more. She'd know what it was he wished to discuss with her.

"Mary," she said urgently some moments later, "please hurry." The maid was taking an inordinate amount of time with the pins, and Kate nearly groaned in frustration. But then, as she turned in her chair, she caught sight of movement beyond her window. Someone was at Ben's castle. Standing, she went to the window as Mary trailed her with the pot of pins. Kate watched the castle while the maid continued poking her hair until... there. The movement she'd spied was Ben. He pulled one of the thick ropes of ivy away from the stones and cut it loose with one deft motion.

Kate spun and rushed from the room as Mary followed, the maid's steps hastening as she strove to keep pace. "Miss Parker! Your hair!" Dimly, Kate realized her hair was only half up, but she couldn't care. Ben was removing the ivy, and she had to stop him.

———

KATE WAS OUT of breath by the time she arrived at Ben's castle. Branches had caught at her skirts as she raced along, and she feared she looked a proper sight. She pulled a leaf from her hair as she came into the castle's clearing. It was empty, and there was no sign of her betrothed.

"Ben!" She skirted a thicket of wild roses to enter the clearing more fully. The castle rose above her, its pale stone peeking through the thick vines that covered the structure. Ben hadn't removed all of it. Not yet, at any rate.

"Kate?"

She turned to see him approaching from the castle's far side. His dark hair was in disarray, and he'd abandoned his neckcloth again. Her heart skipped, and it was with effort that she held her gaze above the exposed skin of his throat.

"What's wrong? Has something happened?" He

hurried to her side. His eyes took in her hair, and she could understand why he might assume something was amiss.

She shook her head, still a bit breathless from her dash. "I saw you from my window. Why are you removing the ivy?"

His lips quirked in amusement. "You came all this way to ask me about the ivy?"

"You can't take it down." She pressed a hand to her throat as she pulled in another breath. "Please, don't take it down."

His brow furrowed as he took her hand and led them to a low wall. He settled them both atop the stones and studied their joined hands. "I wondered if per'aps 'tis time to finish the castle."

"To finish—? But it's lovely just as it is."

"I appreciate the sentiment, but 'lovely' is not the adjective I would have chosen."

"Do you still not see it?" she said. "It's—"

"Perfectly imperfect?"

"Yes!"

"You may set your mind at ease," he said softly. "I'm not removing all of the ivy. I thought to clear some of it away and see what remains to be finished, but," he added with a gentle squeeze of her hand, "I'm beginning to see things a bit differently."

"Oh," she said, surprised at how the gentle

pressure of his fingers took her breath. "That's good to hear."

"Per'aps this is the castle 'twas always meant to be. You wouldn't have liked a shiny, new fortress half as much, would you have?"

"I don't think so."

"That bodes well for us then," he said, "for 'tis a clear fact you're getting a perfectly imperfect husband. It sets my mind at ease to know you're pleased by a few bumps and dents."

Kate shifted on the wall and her skirts caught on the low brambles beneath them. As Ben helped her extricate the muslin from a particularly tenacious thorn, he said, "Per'aps the grounds could use a bit of a trim, though. For safety's sake."

"Perhaps," she conceded, "but not too much."

"Not too much," he promised.

She smiled and returned the pressure of his hand with a squeeze of her own. They sat for some moments in silence, each taking in the lengthening shadows as the sun dipped lower on the horizon. Its rays lit the castle's stones where they peeped through their leafy veil, and the intoxicating aroma of wild roses, warmed by the day's heat, surrounded them. It was idyllic, like a watercolor scene from an old fable, and Kate couldn't think of anywhere she'd rather be.

"Kate," Ben said softly, and she turned to face

him. Her posterior had gone numb from sitting atop the stone wall, but the earnestness of his gaze held her in place. "I know I'm not the husband you might have imagined for yourself, but I'll do everything I can to make you happy."

Kate considered that just a few short days before, neither of them had thought to marry the other. Though she couldn't say she was disappointed with the turn her life had taken, neither could she forget Ben's attempts to speak with her. Nor her earlier musings that perhaps he'd found a lady to court in London. She no longer thought that to be the case, but she had to know for certain. She would have everything laid out between them.

"I believe you will, but I have to ask... is there someone waiting for you? Someone in London, perhaps, who holds your affections?" A fleeting frown creased his brow, and Kate held her breath.

"No, Kate. There is no one else."

CHAPTER TWENTY-FIVE

BEN CONSIDERED KATE'S question and the obvious counter rose swiftly in his mind. Did *she*, perhaps, still hold hopes for someone else? Before he could put the question to her, though, she smiled.

"There is no one else for me, either."

Ben's heart found its rhythm again.

"What will you do about London?" she asked.

Ben had lost count of the number of times he'd entertained that particular question in the past days, but he no longer felt the same anxiety over it. Uncertainty, to be sure, but the paralyzing unease that had held him immobile for so long was fading. "I'm undecided," he said, "but I thought we might talk it through together. I can decline Wilkins' offer and we can remain here if that is your wish."

"My wish?" She pulled back from him though

her hand remained in his. "I've certainly no wish to see you forgo such an opportunity. If it's what you want, that is."

"You would leave Cornwall? I know how much you've grown to love it here." The graceful, velvety scent of wild roses, so much like Kate's own soft fragrance, filled the air around them. It was as if Kate and Cornwall were one and the same, and he wasn't certain they should be parted.

"Ben," she said, and he sensed a bit of exasperation in her tone. "We're to be married. My home will be with you, wherever that may be."

Kate's dark gaze was steady on his as he took in the enormity of her words. They both terrified and warmed him, and he wondered how such opposing emotions could exist within his heart at the same time.

"Will you tell me more about this Tregothnan," she said, "and your discussions with Mr. Wilkins?"

Ben released her and stood, rubbing the back of his neck with his free hand. Slowly, he told her of his earliest correspondence with Wilkins. He paced as he talked of columns and pediments and sash windows, terms she probably had little knowledge of and even less concern for. But despite that, her eyes shone as he spoke.

While he had no doubts that as his wife, Kate would follow wherever he went, none of that mattered if his happiness came at the expense of hers. He stopped his pacing and pulled a hand through his hair. Forcing a slow breath into his lungs, he said, "Tell me truthfully: If I were to accept Wilkins' offer, could you see yourself living in London? D'you think you could be happy there?"

"Yes, I think so."

"If you're not, you need only tell me, and we'll return straightaway to Cornwall."

"I think I should like to visit the parks," she said, "and the theaters."

"You could create a new garden to tend, and we'd be sure to make frequent visits to Kew. I think you would enjoy the glasshouses there."

"It sounds lovely."

He took both of her hands in his as they made plans and speculated on a life in London. She seemed intrigued by the possibilities, which only fueled his own excitement. He was restless, like the sea before a storm, but it wasn't an unpleasant sensation. He and Kate seemed to ignite something in the other, and for the first time in his memory, he felt that his soul transcended the boundaries of his person. He was still Benedick Kimbrell, but he was also part of something larger than himself.

"Perhaps Bronwyn could visit us," she said.

He held a derisive snort and nodded instead.

"And your family, of course. Alys could have her season with us if you'd like." Then he frowned as he was reminded of his brother's *confections*. Clearing his throat, he added, "She's been sharing kisses with my brother, by the by."

Kate stared at him for a long moment before a smile broke across her face. "Daniel?"

"Matthew."

"That will send my grandmother into fits."

"Aye."

And though he'd discussed his situation with her father when they'd addressed the marriage papers, he wished to reassure her: "Lest you think me little more than a charming rogue with no concern for practical matters, you should know I've a small portion from my grandfather." He looked up from their hands to add, "I used some of it for my travels to London but the rest, I've invested. You and our children will not want for anything."

Her brows lifted in unflattering surprise. "Oh! I—that—that is good to know."

"I can see I've shocked you, but there's more to me than my pretty face." He winked and added, "Or my form, though I'm that pleased to have your admiration."

The flush on her cheeks was immediate. Ben would have liked to leave things as they were, but there was one more matter he wished to address.

He'd thought long over it during the night, and he knew Alfie had been correct, though it pained him to admit it. But if his marriage was to work, he must accustom himself to more talking.

To that end, he eyed Kate's hands in his and said, "Can I tell you about my uncle Pedrek?"

———

KATE STILLED AT Ben's question, her heart quickening. His blue eyes mirrored the cloudless sky above, and a breeze the dark curl at his temple. "You were close to him."

He swallowed and resumed his seat, though he didn't relinquish her hand. "I love my own father and brothers, of course, but Pedrek was like a second father to me. You've seen how the Kimbrell family lines can blur a bit."

She nodded knowingly, as she'd often found it difficult to tell where one family ended and another began. It had taken her two springs in Newford to account for all of Ben's brothers.

"And Merryn..." Ben's chest rose as he pulled in a long breath. "Merryn is no less a brother to me than my own. We share an uncommon liking for building things, and my uncle meant to see us trained in the skills we needed." He smiled as if remembering. "He was a hard tutor, though—we had to prove ourselves before he'd allow us to do more than the most menial of tasks. I spent all of my seventh year toting about buckets of nails."

"Was it your uncle who taught you how to design balconies and castles?"

"No. That came later, as I grew older, but he taught us the basics of carpentry and the importance of a straight nail. Slate work and the like. When he died, he'd just begun my instruction in millwork."

"I understand your uncle suffered a fall from the Feather's rooftop?"

He nodded. "'Twas the same year you came to Newford the first time."

"Shortly after your mother passed." This much she knew. She recalled seeing his mother's funeral from her father's carriage—an endless line of dark hats and suits as Ben's relations walked with the coffin to the church.

Kate's family had departed Cornwall soon after for a botany lecture up north, and when they arrived back in Melton Mowbray, she'd had a letter from Bronwyn. Kate's heart had broken again, this time for the friend who'd lost her father. She hadn't known at the time how much of a role Pedrek had played in Ben's life, but to lose both his mother and a beloved uncle so near to one another must have been devastating. It made the carefree mask he wore all the more impressive, and she marveled he hadn't suffocated beneath the weight of it.

"Aye," he said softly. "I wondered if you weren't an angel sent to prepare me—Well."

He paused in his tale, turning his gaze to the valley below, and Kate silently urged him not to stop. Now that he'd started talking about his uncle, she couldn't bear it if he were to close himself to her again. When he continued speaking, she released the breath she'd been holding.

"The day Pedrek died, Merryn was abed with a fever, so 'twas just my uncle and me on the roof." He filled his lungs with a heavy breath, and she sensed the effort his story required. "The truth is, I left my tools where I shouldn't have, and he didn't tie his rope as he ought to have done. 'Twas the makings of a disaster from the start." Ben inhaled, and Kate gripped his hand tighter in hers. "When he fell, I rushed to the edge of the roof, but I wasn't able to pull him up before... well, before."

"Oh, Ben," she whispered. "How truly horrible. I know you carry the weight of his death, but you mustn't. It was a tragic accident."

"Merryn has said much the same, but guilt—'tis like a third leg. You never ask for't, but once there, 'tis a heavy burden to lose. In truth, 'twould be hard to stand without it."

"I'm certain your uncle would want you to find peace in your life," she whispered.

"He would," Ben agreed. He paused, and a small crease appeared between his brows as he considered his words. "But every night before I go to sleep, I relive that day. I hear his boots on the slate. I can't recall how many seconds passed before I knew what was happening. Perhaps if I'd acted more quickly... You deserve a worthy husband, Kate, but I'm afraid the one you're getting is a bit broken."

She swallowed at the earnestness in his gaze. "I think we are all of us a bit chipped and broken about the edges," she said. "Perfectly imperfect in our own way, but every break makes us a bit stronger for it, I think."

"I always knew you were uncommonly wise," he said with the crooked smile she adored.

"I would like to know more of your uncle," she said. "What was he like?"

A bit of the tension eased from Ben's frame and his shoulders relaxed. Kate listened in silence as he spoke, his tone growing lighter with the love he'd had for his uncle. He shared a joke that his uncle had been fond of—something about a turnscrew—and it caused his eyes to crinkle in laughter. In truth, she didn't find the jest all that humorous, but Ben's smile was contagious and she found herself chuckling along with him.

At one point, he stood and put two paces between them. When he lifted a hand to wipe at the moisture on his cheek, Kate felt her own eyes burn for the guilt Ben felt over his uncle's death. He'd been trapped by it, unable to move forward. She ached for him and the boy who'd donned a devil-may-care guise to hide his pain. That he would now open himself to her in such a way caused love to swell in her chest. As she sat with his hand in hers, a curious peace entered her heart. A warm and quiet light, a wholeness that filled her corners.

When his stories wound down, she said softly, "I'm sorry for your uncle's loss and that I never had the chance to know him."

"Thank you," he said.

They looked out over the valley together, at the sun continuing its slow slide toward the horizon. So much had happened in the past days that it all felt a bit surreal. She and Ben had gone swiftly and unexpectedly from friends to something much more, and she felt compelled to say, "So, we are truly betrothed."

———

"WE ARE TRULY betrothed," BEN said. Then, finding his smile, he added, "Did you ever think to find yourself betokened to a common rogue?"

She eyed him, head tilted to one side as she considered his words. Understanding dawned and her eyes widened. "You *were* trying to steal a kiss, all those years before."

"Did you doubt it?"

"Yes. I don't know. Sometimes."

She stood and closed the distance between them in two steps. Her dark eyes were intent on his, and two spots of color stained her cheeks. "But you're wrong about one thing: there is nothing common about you."

"I'm as common as they come," he said with a grin, pleased to have finally played that card. But his heart nearly stopped its momentum at her next words.

"You're hardly that. I knew it from that first spring when you landed in the sea," she said. "You were soaked through, and you grinned up at me—just like that—and you laughed. I've never heard such an *uncommonly* charming sound."

He wasn't sure what to say to that, but Alfie had said he must begin talking more. Surely, his brother didn't mean for him to say *everything* that crossed his mind, but that is what he did.

"Kate," he said, taking her hand in his and drawing her close. "I have loved you from the first."

"And I, you."

There was no hesitation. No frowning consideration or chewing of her lip. There was only certainty. Ben's heart did stop its normal rhythm then, and his breath froze in his chest. Kate gazed at him with such emotion in her eyes that he had no trouble believing her words.

She leaned toward him, and her soft rose fragrance filled the narrow space between them. Her eyes were bright, her lips ripe and pink to match her cheeks. They beckoned him, and he closed the distance, hesitating a hair's breadth from her as he waited for a squirrel to drop a nut onto their heads or the cloudless sky to unleash a sudden torrent. When neither of those happened, he allowed their lips to touch.

It was the blissful peace of coming home after a long journey, only... more. Like the warm comfort of a favorite blanket—but softer—or the burst of a sun-ripened strawberry on the tongue—only sweeter.

Her lips were perfection beneath his, as he knew they would be. Full and bow-shaped and perfectly fitted to his. Their breath mingled and he closed his eyes, bringing one hand to the silken hair at her nape. He traced the gentle curve of her neck while his other hand curled about her waist, pulling her closer. She wound slim fingers through the hair above his collar, her touch sending a shiver across his fevered skin.

Their kiss was everything he expected and nothing he could have imagined. He may have been a fool to expect perfection in his life, but not where kissing Kate was concerned.

CHAPTER TWENTY-SIX

NEWFORD'S INAUGURAL PERFORMANCE of *Much Ado About Nothing* opened to a full house. The benches in front were packed elbow-to-elbow, the lanterns had been turned low, and the rooms behind the stage hummed with low whispers as props were changed out and costumes readied for each scene. Ben had tasked Matthew and Daniel with the mechanism that rotated the balcony, and though he consulted with them frequently, his brothers seemed to have all in order. There'd been nothing for him to do but play his part.

The ladies had trussed him in silk knee breeches, a brocade waistcoat and shoes with shiny buckles. Someone had deemed it a brilliant notion to adorn his perfectly respectable top hat with a feather. As if that weren't enough to lower a man's consequence, a lace cravat—lace!—formed an impenetrable barrier between him and his dignity, but at least his cousins sported equally mortifying costumes.

As Leonato, Gavin wore yellow pantaloons—Ben couldn't stop his snort at that—and carried a lion-headed walking stick. His waistcoat had been done in an exceptionally loud damask, a pattern that looked remarkably like some curtains Ben had seen once in Morwenna's shop. Cadan, despite his role as the soldier Claudio, fared little better with a tall shako hat and broad epaulets that were more farce than fashion. Ben found comfort in their shared disgrace.

It was the fifth act, and as he readied himself for the play's final scenes, Kate eyed his cravat. Owing to his poor handling of the thing—the blasted lace was scratchy—it had begun to wilt somewhere around the end of the first act.

"Here," she said as she took up the ends. "You've made a hash of it."

He looked down, frowning, and she tipped his chin back up with one finger. They stood close enough he could see the shadow of her lashes on her cheeks and breathe in the soft rose scent of her hair. Close enough that if he leaned forward just the merest bit, he could kiss her neck. Or perhaps he'd press his lips to the soft shell of her ear... or the tiny freckle next to her mouth.

It was fair to say they'd shared a number of kisses

since their afternoon at the folly just days before. Each one had had its own tenor, from swift and chaste to long and leisurely to heated and fervent. The notion that he was to have an entire lifetime of Kate's kisses still left him a bit staggered.

"Not now," Kate whispered, divining his thoughts. She continued to unravel the knot at his throat with deft fingers, and his frown returned.

"How the devil"—he cleared his throat and began again. "How d'you know how to tie a man's cravat?"

With a press of her lips that told him she was fighting a smile, she said, "I've tied enough for my father that I think I can manage the effort. Though I have to say, my father's cravats have never had such an abundance of lace. It just wants a bit of courage to master the folds."

Ben scoffed. "'Tis amusing that you pair courage with a lace cravat, though to be sure, it requires an excess of the one to don the other."

"Your brothers and cousins must be envious," she said without even the hint of a smile.

Before he could form a proper response to that bit of nonsense, Bronwyn's head appeared in the open doorway. "'Tis almost the final scene, Ben. We'll be needed on the stage soon."

He closed his eyes as Kate finished her knot. He and Bronwyn had agreed, after much debate, to a chaste cheek-kiss to conclude the play's final act. The sooner they got the matter over with, the better, as far as he was concerned, though he was certain his cousin meant to wring as much drama from the scene as she could.

"Your hat, Benedick," Kate said.

He opened his eyes and settled the feathered top hat on his head with a rakish tilt.

"You wear it with distinction." She wore such a look of innocence that he wondered, briefly, if his own betrothed hadn't had a hand in his humiliation.

"Ben," Bronwyn said again, this time more urgently.

"I'm coming." He directed his gaze to the mirror, made a final adjustment to the lace at his throat, and turned to go.

As he went, Kate whispered, "Kiss me later," in his ear, which did nothing for his concentration.

———

KATE'S CHEEKS WERE still warm as she watched Ben go, but beneath her giddiness—which had been worthy of one of Alys's novels in recent days—was an unease she couldn't name. Ben looked magnificent as Shakespeare's Benedick, though the feather was a bit over the top. It had been Bronwyn's notion, and though Kate had offered disagreement, her protests hadn't been very loud.

But she and Ben were to be married. They were to form a single unit, bound by their love for one another as they faced the world together. It was only a feather, but she ought to have been stronger in her support of him.

Her grandmother's words returned to her, as they'd done repeatedly since the afternoon of Kate's unexpected betrothal. Though many of their acquaintances claimed they'd long predicted Kate and Ben's union, she wondered if others were of a same mind as Lady Catherine. As Mrs. Pentreath and the matrons. Did they assume Kate married Ben solely because circumstances required it? It was true that their poorly timed rehearsal had hastened things along, but their love for one another was undeniable. Given time, she liked to think they might have found their own way to altar.

And that, she realized, was the source of her unease. That anyone should think they married out of necessity rather than love. Or worse: that *Ben* should ever think it. In less than two weeks, they would declare themselves before God and man, but it wasn't enough. She paced the small dressing room, her unease growing until inspiration struck.

The idea was a bold one. Could she manage it? Yes, she thought, drawing a deep breath. Her hands shook a bit and her stomach knotted more than a bit, but her love for Ben was fortifying. The strength it gave her—a little terrifying. But it was inspiring and emboldening all the same. She could do this.

"Bronwyn," she called as she hurried from the room. She found her friend before the other dressing mirror, lifting the veil she'd wear for the final scene. "How long before you must join the others?" Kate asked.

Bronwyn studied her in confusion before her expression gave way to a wide smile. "Just long enough, I should think."

———

KATE'S PARTING WORDS were sufficiently distracting that Ben barely noticed the crowd gathered on their benches as he returned to the stage, but somehow his brain led him to his place. It continued to see him through as he delivered his lines, though he'd not recall later if he'd done them properly. Finally, he found his mark at one side of the balcony and awaited Bronwyn's entrance for the final scene, but she didn't come.

The audience shifted, and he peered into the shadows, but they were empty. Was his cousin having trouble navigating the balcony's stairs? He thought he'd made them wide enough to accommodate the ladies' skirts.

Cadan quirked an inquiring brow at him as whispers rose across the theater. Ben turned back to the audience and cleared his throat. "Forsooth," he said in wry improvisation, "let not the march of time erode our hope, for true love knows not minutes nor hours."

Gavin in his yellow pantaloons held back a smile as laughter rippled through the audience. Ben searched his mind for something else to say while they awaited Bronwyn. And to think, she'd been prodding *him* along! She'd have done better to direct her efforts toward her own preparations.

He considered what the Bard himself might say in such a situation. "In its truest guise," he continued, "love doth bloom in its own season, without concern for clocks and schedules. But, dear audience, is the blossom not worth the wait?"

There were murmurs and chuckles from the benches, though Mrs. P, seated on the first row, frowned in disapproval. Finally, a voice spoke softly behind him.

"I am here, Benedick."

His heart stilled and he turned slowly. The figure before him was veiled, but he recognized his betrothed's voice. The tilt of her head and the smooth lines of her form. The hands clasped tightly before her, most likely to still their shaking. He would recognize her anywhere, so often had he seen her in his dreams.

Kate wore his cousin's costume, a dark burgundy gown with a high ruffled neckline and puffed sleeves. He swallowed as she slowly lifted the lacy veil to reveal herself. Cadan and Gavin's brows lifted in matching expressions of surprise, and Miss Carew smiled broadly. The audience quieted at this unexpected twist.

The rich gown brought out the sumptuous brown of her eyes and the high color in her cheeks. Her hair remained as it had been, the tresses smooth and softly piled at the back of her head, but she'd added combs adorned with pearls.

Her gaze was soft as she eyed him, and he extended one hand to draw her forward.

She leaned close to whisper, "We never finished our rehearsal."

Ben's heart beat a heavy rhythm in his chest. He couldn't help the grin that broke across his face. "Miss Parker, is this your way of stealing a kiss?"

"Aye," she said in whispered imitation of him.

Encouraged by the light in her eyes, he lifted his brows in roguish reply. "You needn't resort to thievery."

"I should hope not."

The audience moved about restlessly as they waited for the scene to continue, so with a final nod for Kate, he lifted his voice and began.

BEN AS BENEDICK (to Beatrice): Do not you love me?

KATE AS BEATRICE (grinning): Why no, no more than reason.

BENEDICK: Why then, your uncle and the Prince and Claudio have been deceived. They swore you did.

BEATRICE: Do not you love me?

BENEDICK: Troth, no, no more than reason.

BEATRICE: Why then, my cousin, Margaret, and Ursula are much deceived, for they did swear you did.

BENEDICK: They swore that you were almost sick for me.

BEATRICE: They swore that you were well-nigh dead for me.

GAVIN AS LEONATO (with a meaningful eye toward Kate): Come, I am sure you love the gentleman.

A hush had befallen the audience by now. Ben's eyes remained on Kate's. A smile teased the corner of her mouth as Cadan continued the scene.

CLAUDIO: And I'll be sworn upon 't that he loves her, for here's a paper written in his hand, a halting sonnet of his own pure brain, fashioned to Beatrice.

MISS CAREW AS HERO (producing a letter with a grand flourish): And here's another, writ in my cousin's hand, stol'n from her pocket, containing her affection unto Benedick.

BENEDICK (to Beatrice): A miracle! Here's our own hands against our hearts. Come, I will have thee, but by this light I take thee for pity.

BEATRICE: I would not deny you, but by this good day, I yield upon great persuasion.

Ben's heart thumped so heavily he thought it must be heard by all. Kate waited for him to deliver his final line, and he felt her anticipation keenly. It vibrated in the air about them, but more than her anticipation, he felt her love for him. He was certain everyone in the theater could sense it, and the notion caused pride to rush through him, that she would declare her choice so plainly. Her eyes as she studied him were dark and fathomless. He could happily drown in them, but the audience was restless, so he said the words.

"Peace! I will stop your mouth."

He lowered his head and touched Kate's lips with his. Her mouth was soft, her lips warm and welcoming, and he pulled her to him. He inhaled the scent of her and lifted one hand to stroke the petal softness of her cheek. Everything and everyone disappeared—the stage, their fellow actors, the audience—as he reveled in the wondrous sensation of holding Kate in his arms.

For years, he'd lamented his poor timing—from his first attempts to steal a kiss from Kate to their fateful near-kiss on this very stage just days before. But his timing, it seemed, had been right all along. It was just as it should have been to bring them to this moment. He might have continued kissing Kate indefinitely if not for Bronwyn's surprised exclamation.

"Mrs. P has fainted!"

EPILOGUE

KIMBRELL'S FOLLY
TWENTY YEARS LATER

"IT'S PERFECT, PAPA." Beth clutched Ben's arm through the wool of his coat as she'd always done whenever she became overexcited. "It's simply breathtaking, and I can't imagine a better setting for my wedding breakfast."

Ben lifted a doubtful brow at this, but he patted his daughter's hand anyway. He thought *breathtaking* might have been a kindness for the crumbling pile, but he couldn't deny the view high above Newford's quilted valley was something to behold.

"Oh, look. Here's Morwenna now," Beth said. She dropped Ben's arm with unflattering haste and left him. He couldn't imagine what more there was to discuss regarding his daughter's wedding breakfast, but clearly there were lists that must be checked and contingencies to be made. He'd designed entire mansions with less elaborate schemes, and they'd turned out fine.

A soft hand curled into his as Kate took Beth's place. Her wide skirts rustled against his trousers as she pressed close to him. "Beth is pleased with the work on the castle?"

He smiled. "Our daughter has a liking for the perfectly imperfect, just like her mother."

A warm breeze tossed about the heady scent of roses as they gazed on Kimbrell's Folly. The stone walls were still covered in thick twists of ivy and wild roses, but the wildness had been brought to heel somewhat, at least to the point of safety for their guests. A team of gardeners had been called in to trim the worst of the overgrowth, dutifully heeding Kate and Beth's warnings of "Not too much!"

Ben had also seen to the structure itself, engaging Merryn's firm to make repairs to the tower, which had begun to lean a bit. Although the rafters had become home to a colony of bats over the years, at least their guests wouldn't be struck by falling stones as they strolled the picturesque grounds.

Despite Kate's loyalty—for she still only referred to it as a castle—the citizens of Newford had long and infallible memories. His castle would always be known as Kimbrell's Folly, and as he gazed on its weathered stones and crumbling battlements, he couldn't argue the name. It *was*, in the strictest of terms, a garden folly after all. Ornamental and whimsical. Impractical in the extreme, but beautiful in its imperfections. He was hard pressed to recall the man who'd once cringed to look upon it.

But the folly wasn't the only thing of interest on this particular ridge. Some distance from the castle's easternmost corner, a small statue of pale white marble overlooked the valley. A silent sentry in the figure of St. Thomas, patron saint of builders. Shortly after he and Kate had wed, she'd suggested the statue as a memorial to Ben's uncle, and he found solace in looking on it whenever they returned to Cornwall.

That Beth had insisted on having her wedding breakfast here was no mystery as his eldest had always had a delighted fascination for the folly. Of all their children, she was the most like Kate in that regard. They'd been blessed with six children in all, though two had preceded them from this life. Their loss was an ache that never left, but it was tempered by the joys he and Kate found in every day.

Ben had spent three more years learning his craft with Wilkins and two years of study at the Royal Academy Schools before setting out his own shingle. Since then, he'd designed everything from schools to hospitals to a hunting lodge for their new queen.

And of course, an elegant glasshouse for his wife so she might always have flowers about. Though she would always prefer the perfectly imperfect wildflowers of Cornwall, she'd been very appreciative of his efforts.

Some of his designs had been received with acclaim, others with criticism. The acclaim he liked, especially when it came from the queen herself. The criticism he preferred to avoid, although he'd learned that was a foolish and futile hope. And if he withdrew occasionally to hold his emotions close, Kate had a way of teasing them out of him. She always knew just the thing to say to ease his heart.

Now, though, it seemed she needed some easing of her own as she said softly, "Our daughter will leave us soon."

Something tightened in Ben's chest, and he placed his hand over Kate's as they watched Beth and Morwenna strategize over seating arrangements or some such. Given the number of Ben's relations, it would require the precision of a military campaign to see them all seated properly, so perhaps their excessive planning wasn't without merit.

"I know we can't keep her with us forever," Kate added with a gentle sniff, "but another year or two wouldn't have hurt anything. I was three and twenty when you and I wed."

"Aye, a teasy old maid," he confirmed. A bit of

the tension left Kate's frame at his teasing, and she leaned into him. He gathered her against his side and added more seriously, "'Tis a fact our story moved at a different pace than Beth's, but we'll endure. A wise lady once told me every break makes us stronger."

"Hmm. She does sound wise. Perhaps you should have married her."

He smiled. "Bear up, love. With a bit of grace and good fortune, we'll soon have grandchildren to hold on our knees."

Her expression lightened at that and she smiled. "You always know just the thing to say to ease my heart."

To be sure, their lives had not been perfect. They'd suffered loss and disappointment but untold joys and peace as well. And each break *had* made them stronger. His wife truly was the most profound lady of his acquaintance.

THE END

Thank you for reading! If you enjoyed Kate and Ben's tale, be sure to claim your copy of the series prequel novella at klynsmithauthor.com. Discovering Wynne is free to newsletter subscribers!

AUTHOR'S NOTE

I create a mood board of the visual references I use when writing. If you would like to see my inspiration for Ben, Kate and their environs, please check out https://www.pinterest.com/klynsmithauthor/kissing-kate/.

Kissing Kate is a book of fiction based on events, attitudes and practices of the period. Below are a few themes that influenced this story.

*** SPOILERS AHEAD ***

Architecture. In the early 19th century, the path to becoming an architect was not as clearly defined as it is today. Many gentlemen mastered the craft through apprenticeships or self-study. This era saw the emergence of notable architects like Thomas Allom (1804-1872), a visionary whose early career served as inspiration for Ben's path. Allom, the son of a coachman from Suffolk, apprenticed to established architect Francis Goodwin before studying at the Royal Academy School.

Much Ado About Nothing. In crafting Ben and Kate's story, I delved into the world of Regency-era theater productions and found inspiration in the timeless play, *Much Ado About Nothing*. Written by William Shakespeare in the late 16th century and retold countless times on stage and screen, this comedy revolves around themes of love and the complexities of human relationships, among others. Its plot is very different from *Kissing Kate*, but the masks which often conceal the characters' true identities may be seen as parallels to the masks Kate and Ben wear. Fans and students of Shakespeare will recognize that the lines included from Act 5, Scene 4 have been shortened slightly for the purpose of brevity.

Theater Productions. Village theater productions were a significant source of entertainment and community engagement in the Regency era. These performances were typically held in local assembly rooms, barns, or other venues, and the plays ranged from Shakespearean classics to contemporary comedies.

Sets were generally comprised of wooden frames and painted backdrops that represented the various scenes required for the play. Many of the innovations common to the larger urban theaters—trapdoors, hidden compartments, and rotating panels—were not commonly used in village productions due to the constraints of space and resources. I love the creativity and resourcefulness

Ben shows in this story with his rotating balcony set and the use of the fishermen's sails as backdrops.

Trauma & Grief. Writing believable trauma into a fictional narrative is hard. It requires balancing the historical context with the complexities of human emotion. In 19th century England, the understanding and treatment of grief and trauma were vastly different from contemporary approaches. Society's comprehension of psychological and emotional distress was limited, and the prevailing attitude was often one of stoicism and restraint.

As for trauma, the term as we understand it today didn't exist, and there was little awareness of post-traumatic stress or the psychological toll of traumatic events. Instead, individuals were encouraged to cope with their experiences privately, with few outlets for seeking help or support.

Grief, trauma, and guilt can have a significant impact on an individual's emotional state, as well as memory and cognitive processes. In Ben's case, the tragic event of his uncle's fall and his perception of his own role in it made it challenging for him to recall the specific details of his uncle's lesson. It also played a role in Ben's perfectionism, which can be a coping strategy to mask feelings of vulnerability and insecurity.

If you or someone you know is experiencing the effects of trauma or struggling with grief, there are numerous resources available worldwide to provide support. Consider reaching out to mental health professionals, counselors, or therapists who specialize in trauma and grief therapy. You can also explore local or international organizations, such as those dedicated to mental health and well-being. Additionally, seek out support groups or community organizations in your area, as they can offer valuable guidance and assistance tailored to your specific location.

BOOKS BY K. LYN SMITH

Something Wonderful
The Astronomer's Obsession
The Footman's Tale (Short Story)*
The Artist's Redemption
The Physician's Dilemma

Hearts of Cornwall
Discovering Wynne (Prequel Novella)*
Jilting Jory
Matching Miss Moon
Driving Miss Darling
Kissing Kate

Love's Journey
Star of Wonder
Light of a Nile Moon

* Subscribe at klynsmithauthor.com for these free bonuses!

ABOUT THE AUTHOR

K. Lyn Smith's heart resides in Birmingham, Alabama, where she writes sweet historical romance about ordinary people finding extraordinary love. Her debut novel, The Astronomer's Obsession, was a finalist for the National Excellence in Romantic Fiction Award, while many of her other titles have been shortlisted for honors such as the American Writing Award, the Carolyn Reader's Choice Award, the HOLT Medallion and the Maggie Award. When she's not lost in the pages of a book, you can find her with family, traveling to far-off places and binging period dramas. And space documentaries. Weird, right?

Visit www.klynsmithauthor.com, where you can subscribe for new release updates and access to exclusive bonus content.

Printed in the USA
CPSIA information can be obtained
at www.ICGtesting.com
JSHW020515241023
50728JS00006B/22